YOURS FOR CHRISTMAS

A ROYALLY UNEXPECTED CHRISTMAS

LILIAN MONROE

Cover photo by Regina Wamba
Cover design by Mayhem Cover Creations
Editing by Shavonne Clarke

WANT THREE BOOKS DELIVERED STRAIGHT TO YOUR INBOX?
HOW ABOUT THREE ROCK STAR ROMANCES THAT WERE WAY TOO
HOT TO SELL?

GET THE COMPLETE *ROCK HARD* SERIES:
WWW.LILIANMONROE.COM/ROCKHARD

1

ADA

My gown flows like liquid silver over my skin. Glancing up at my sisters as I enter the living room, I spread my palms. "What do you think?" Giving them an awkward smile, I run my fingers over the silky fabric.

"When did you get so pretty?" my younger sister Kiera asks. She pushes her thick-rimmed glasses further up her nose, her other hand still poised over the laptop on her thighs. "Even when you dress up for your piano performances, you never look this good."

"Is that supposed to be a compliment?" I grin, rolling my eyes.

"You look gorgeous, Ada," Maggie says. My older sister's eyes are soft, and her dark hair is pulled back in a smooth, sleek ponytail at the nape of her neck. Even with a gray air cast strapped all the way up to her mid-calf and her broken ankle propped up on the couch in front of her, she still manages to look put together. With a cashmere cardigan draped over her shoulders and a simple string of pearls around her neck, she is every bit a duchess.

She should be the one wearing this gown, not me.

"I wish you hadn't broken your ankle." I sigh. "You've never had an accident dancing before."

My sister, gracefully reclined on the chaise, gives me a soft smile. Only slight tension around her eyes betrays how much her injury bothers her. "I'll be dancing again in no time. The Farcliff Ballet Company has assured me they'll support my recovery for as long as it takes. Plus, it's been years since you've attended a royal event. It's your turn."

"My turn to endure the drudgery?" I pop an eyebrow.

Maggie's smile tugs, her noble façade shimmering for a moment. "Your turn to enjoy yourself," she corrects.

I nod, shifting my weight from foot to foot. I bite my lip, only remembering after a moment that it's painted bright red, and I've probably smeared my lipstick all over my teeth.

A graceful duchess I am not.

Reading my body language, Maggie smiles. "You'll be great, Ada. You have every right to be at the castle in my place, and you'll make a wonderful impression on the King and Queen."

"Will I, though? I do have that whole foot-in-mouth syndrome, where I blurt out the wrong thing at the worst possible time."

Maggie grins, shaking her head. "It's all in your head. Everyone loves you. Say hello to Count Gregory for me."

My lips turn down. "Are you sure you still want to marry him?" I ask. "He's twice your age."

"It's a good match," Maggie answers. She glances at Kiera, whose nose is firmly pressed against her computer screen.

Maggie's upcoming betrothal to Count Gregory is a good match because it will elevate our family's standing. Count Gregory is well-connected, especially with universities and colleges in the Kingdom. He's a benefactor to a number of research institutions and has the ear of most deans and university directors on the continent.

So, if Maggie marries Count Gregory, it will give Kiera the opportunity to attend the best university in Farcliff Kingdom at the tender age of fifteen. Our little sister is a bona fide genius, and she deserves the best.

It's just that our family's position has slipped somewhat in the past couple of decades, and *the best* isn't exactly available to her without this marriage.

My grandfather made some bad business decisions, and my parents care more about art than they do about money. Simply put, we don't have the cash to put her through university. Doing so would require selling the Belcourt Estate, which would strip us of our titles and standing.

Maggie marrying Count Gregory would solve a lot of issues. But—*ugh*. He's *old*. Judging by the pictures I've seen, he wouldn't be Maggie's first choice for a husband. He wouldn't even be my last choice. Wouldn't make the list.

We're the type of royals who, if we happen to end up in a tabloid or magazine, need an explanation following our names. Not exactly A-list celebrities, but enough royal blood to make us noteworthy on a slow news day.

My grandfather was the former King's younger brother. Grandpa had seven children, the youngest of which is my father. So I suppose the current King is my second cousin. Or is it first cousin once removed? I don't know. The family tree is sprawling, and the reigning monarch and I are on opposite sides. I'm currently one hundred and twelfth in the line of succession, after Maggie.

I don't get recognized in the street, is what I'm saying, but I do get called *Lady Belcourt* when I go to official events. Which is rarely, by the way.

We're the type of royals who need to work—albeit we

have bourgeois, aristocratic jobs. My parents run an art gallery in Farcliff City, Maggie is a ballet dancer, and I'm a concert pianist. We're not plastering walls for a living, but we aren't spending all our time doing charity, either. In the pecking order of royals, the Belcourts are solidly on the bottom rung.

I'm not holding my breath as I wait for my chance to sit on the throne. I've successfully avoided royal responsibilities.

Until now.

As I try to stuff down the fluttering nerves in my belly, I turn to see my mother and father walking through the living room doorway. My mother is in her finest gown, a simple, elegant black taffeta dress. My father, in his crisp tuxedo, rubs his hand over his freshly-shaven face. His hair, now entirely gray, is combed back in a sleek yet effortless style.

The Duke and Duchess of Belcourt.

They don't look like members of the royal family hanging onto a tenuous relationship to their land and titles. They look completely at ease with themselves and with our destination this evening.

Our destination being Farcliff Castle, for the annual Royal Christmas Ball.

This year, the entire Kingdom is coming. It's the new heir's first Christmas. His Highness Prince Charlie is the first child of the new King and Queen. There was some controversy with King Charlie taking the throne beside a commoner, Queen Elle, but I personally adore them. They thumbed their nose at tradition and followed love.

Unlike Maggie, who will need to marry crotchety old Count Gregory to make sure our little sister can go to college.

Everyone who's anyone is going to the ball to welcome the young heir into the world. Everyone, including my parents and me—even though I'm not sure we qualify as people who matter.

I clear my throat, trying to hide my nerves. I've only been to the castle once in the past ten years, at which time I told the former King that I liked his mustache, but had he ever considered dyeing it so it matched his hair?

Foot-in-mouth, remember?

Reading my mind, Maggie smiles at me, pulling me from my thoughts. She dips her chin down as if to say, *You'll be fine. Stop worrying.*

Kiera gasps, looking up from her laptop. "The Duke of Blythe is attending." Her fingers fly over the keyboard, presumably to pull up every available photo and live stream of the ball. Her cheek turns pink as her eyes bug out. "He looks so *hot.*"

"Kiera," Mother chides, pinching her lips. "That's no way for a lady to speak."

"It's the truth," my little sister replies, spinning the laptop around. A photo of the reclusive Duke of Blythe stares back at me, and my knees go weak. Even in an unposed, unedited paparazzi photo, Kiera's right. He looks more than human, like he was made just a little too perfect to be real. His eyes are an impossibly complicated shade of green, like the color of a forest canopy in midsummer. His strong, chiseled jaw looks sharp enough to slice the laptop screen open.

Unlike my father, the Duke has chosen to keep a smattering of stubble over the lower half of his face. I don't know why that makes my stomach clench.

The Duke inherited everything when his parents passed away four years ago, but everyone says he's ruining himself and his estate. His parents were well-known musicians who started one of the finest piano-making businesses in the world. They hired all the best artisans and made Blythe

Pianos famous worldwide. I've only ever played a Blythe piano once in my life, but I still remember the way it felt and sounded—incredible.

By all accounts, the Duke of Blythe spent the last four years running the family business into the ground. A little stubble on his jaw is the least of his worries.

Clearing my throat, I turn away from the screen and force a smile at my mother. "Ready?"

She extends a gloved hand toward me, giving me a soft smile. "You look beautiful, Ada."

"Ada!" Kiera calls out behind me. I turn around to see a wicked, cheeky grin on her face. "Get a selfie with the Duke of Blythe and tell me if he's as perfect in person as he is in photos. I bet he smells amazing."

Kiera's cheeks are red, her eyes shining with the energy of a young teenager. She stares at me expectantly as my mother makes a disapproving noise, but I can't quite hide my smile.

"I'll see what I can do," I answer, earning an even louder disapproving noise from Mother.

My little sister squeals, throwing her laptop to the side and jumping up to give me a hug. She stops short at the last second, holding up her hands. "Don't want to ruin your dress."

I blow her a kiss. "I'll get you a picture."

Kiera smiles wider. "Thanks. The girls at school are so in love with him. Did you know he hasn't left the Blythe Estate in over a year? They say he gets women delivered there along with all his food."

"Kiera, that's enough," Mother snaps. "The Duke of Blythe values his privacy, and it's completely inappropriate and unbecoming for you to be spreading nasty rumors about him. We all know what he's been through. I wouldn't want to leave my castle, either."

6

Kiera pouts. "I heard his brother—"

"Enough." My mother's voice leaves no room for protest.

Kiera drops her chin, but flicks her eyes up to mine. There's no remorse in them, only a deep, bubbling curiosity.

I grin. I suppose if I were fifteen, I'd be interested in a man like the Duke of Blythe, too.

The Duke is shrouded in controversy. His younger brother passed away four years ago, and they say his parents died of a broken heart shortly afterward. Within six months, the Duke lost his brother and both his parents and inherited the lands, titles, the business, and responsibility of the dukedom.

It caused ripples in Farcliff high society.

Those poor parents. No one should have to see their children die, old ladies would whisper. Then, *I heard it was an overdose.*

Judgment and sympathy, so tightly intertwined it's impossible to tell the difference between the two. His brother was a drug addict who overdosed, and his parents couldn't take the heartbreak. Or maybe the shame.

And the new Duke of Blythe?

He retreated. Brooding, unreachable, and attractive enough to make him interesting. Schoolgirls all over Farcliff are obsessed with him—Kiera being one of them.

Right now, I appreciate him if only for the fact that it'll give me something to do while I'm at the stuffy, pretentious Royal Christmas Ball.

Operation: Get A Selfie With A Reclusive Duke has begun.

I grin at my sister, then do my best to school my features before turning around to nod at my parents. "Let's go."

2

ADA

As my parents and I get in the town car that will take us to the castle, I let out a long breath.

My mother reaches over to pat my thigh, giving me a tight smile. "It'll be fine, Ada. Just be yourself. Your father and I appreciate you stepping into your sister's shoes tonight."

My father glances back at me from the front seat, his icy blue eyes deathly serious. "Count Gregory will no doubt be disappointed that he won't get to speak to Maggie, but I trust you'll do your best to make a good impression."

I give him a quick glance. "Of course."

"His marriage to Maggie is important," my mother adds.

Shifting my faux-fur wrap tighter around my shoulders, I nod. "I understand."

My gut churns uncomfortably. It's not fair that Maggie has to marry a man like Count Gregory. She doesn't get to fall in love or choose someone she loves. For our family, she has to sacrifice her chance at a loving relationship.

It's not to say that Count Gregory would never love her, or she him. I've never met the man. He could be lovely. But it's just the *principle* that bothers me. My sister is a prima ballerina, gorgeous and willowy and intelligent, and she has to marry a man who's done nothing but live off his family's wealth. He donates to universities, sure, and is well-connected with basically every educational institution in the Kingdom, but still. That doesn't necessarily make him a loving husband.

This isn't a Jane Austen novel. It's the twenty-first century. It shouldn't be happening.

Staring out the window, I turn my attention to the snow-covered countryside. It takes about forty-five minutes to drive into the city from the Belcourt Estate, and I take that time to admire the Kingdom. Farcliff is located between Canada and the United States, to the east of the Great Lakes. This time of year, the last weekend of November, it's cold and snowy and incredibly beautiful. It feels like the whole world has been blanketed in white, with only our black car carving a path through the silent countryside.

We drive through a forest of pines, their branches heavy with fresh snow. Spiny, leafless trees stick out between them, each slender branch topped with its own layer of white. When the city looms up ahead and the trees give way to buildings, my nerves heighten.

It's silly, really. I shouldn't be nervous. I'm a performer. I've played piano in front of packed concert halls. I have no problem being on stage, seated in front of a gleaming instrument, playing music that I've spent hours practicing.

But this? Being in the castle, surrounded by wealth and prestige and dukes and duchesses and even the *King and Queen*?

What if I forget how to curtsy? I could trip and spill red wine all over the Queen's dress. Am I supposed to call the Queen "Her Royal Majesty" or just "Her Majesty?" Will there be dancing? Maggie is the dancer in the family. My feet are only good for jogging and pressing the pedals on my grand piano.

Deep breaths, Ada.

I need to relax, but my heart thuds until I feel my phone buzz in my clutch. I pull it out to see a photo of my sisters and...a printed photo of the Duke of Blythe. Kiera is pretending to kiss the Duke's lips, the sheet of paper crinkling against her face. Maggie laughs beside her.

A message follows: ***Don't forget the selfie.***

My nerves ease, and my lips tug up into a soft smile. I answer: ***I'm on it.***

When my phone buzzes again, I expect to see another message from Kiera. Instead, a daily reminder to take my birth control pops up. Thank goodness I keep extras in every purse. I pop a tiny pill in my mouth, swallowing it down as inconspicuously as I can.

The familiar action settles my nerves the tiniest bit. It's just one evening, and it'll be fine.

Right?

THE TALL, wrought-iron gates leading to Farcliff Castle are open when we arrive, wrapped in silver-and-gold tinsel with a thousand twinkling Christmas lights wound around each spire. The long drive leading up to the entrance is packed full of cars, each more luxurious than the last. There's a Bentley in front of us and a Rolls Royce behind, and suddenly our town car seems a little too ordinary.

Another reminder we don't quite belong.

Farcliff Castle looks like something out of a dream. It shoots up into the sky, all towers and stone, with a thousand windows throwing out golden light. A massive Christmas tree stands tall in the middle of the circular drive, at least a hundred feet tall. It's covered in the most intricate baubles and decorations I've ever seen, with a bright star shining up top.

Strings of lights extend from the tree to lampposts around the drive, so it feels like the stars are dripping down around us. My breath catches, and all of a sudden I'm wrapped up in the beauty of it all. I don't feel like an outsider right now, I just feel like a little girl about to meet Santa Claus.

When a footman opens the door and helps me out of the vehicle, he treats me with the exact same deference as everyone else. "Lady Belcourt," he says with a bow, and I wonder how many hours he's spent studying pictures of all of tonight's attendees. "Please," he says, leading me up the stairs.

Two other footmen help my mother and father out of the car, and I take the first step up the wide marble staircase to the doors. There's a rich red carpet laid out, its edges inlaid with gold thread.

Everything oozes elegance and wealth and holiday spirit. A massive wreath hangs above the door, and when I pass under it another thrill pierces my gut.

I'm at Farcliff Castle. I'm wearing a long silver gown, and my inky black hair is styled to perfection. Even if I feel like an imposter, how could I not enjoy this?

Another member of the royal staff greets me, giving me a slight curtsy as she asks for my jacket. I strip the white faux-fur off my shoulders, tugging the ends of my long gloves off and handing them to her. Holding my clutch close to my stomach, I turn to wait for my mother and father.

The three of us are led in a long procession of people toward the main ballroom, where a delicate, classical rendition of a Christmas song is being played. My nerves relax ever so slightly at the comforting sounds of a violin, a cello, and I think I hear a flute and a piano, too.

I can do this. I can attend this ball and act like a lady and make a good impression on Count Gregory. I can make my parents proud and do right by my sister, even if she can't be here herself.

My insecurities are just that—insecurities. My family is still called Belcourt, and the King is still my second cousin (or first cousin once removed...or whatever). I have as much right to be here as everyone else, even if I didn't arrive in a Rolls Royce.

But when I step through the tall archway into the ballroom, the air is ripped from my lungs. This is beyond opulent. Beyond beautiful. Beneath my high-heeled shoes, the polished floor is inlaid with intricate designs made from semi-precious stones. Tall columns hold up an arching roof, where four massive chandeliers drip with crystals and lights above our heads.

Garlands of pine and tinsel are strung up around the room, with gold and red and silver wrapped around the branches.

And the people.

Oh, my goodness. Silk and sequins. Fine, tailored tuxedos. Diamonds and pearls and emeralds on every earlobe and neck and finger. Literally everything is glittering.

A waiter presents me a tray full of champagne, and I take a flute with a nod. "Thank you," I whisper, my voice hoarse. I don't normally drink, but I feel the need to do something with my hands. Hold something. Help the illusion that I belong here. As my mother and father trail in behind me, I've already finished the drink. Oops. A waiter whisks it away without me having to ask.

My mother's hand appears on my elbow. "There's the Count," she says, nodding to a tall older man across the room. "We should say hello."

I nod, letting my mother and father flank me on either side. My eyes are still adjusting to the twinkling jewels and richness in the room when I feel a prickling on the back of my neck. The sensation turns to a warm rush that spreads down my spine, bathing my body in heat.

In the opposite corner of the ballroom to where Count Gregory is standing is the Duke of Blythe...

...and he's staring straight at me.

3

HEATH

I DON'T WANT to be here.

Or rather, I didn't until about two seconds ago.

Who...?

I watch a black-haired beauty enter the room, her eyes widening. She stares up at the ceiling, those red, plump lips falling open.

There's a twitch in my pants, and I remember I'm a man. A man who hasn't slept with anyone in far too long, no matter what the tabloids write about me.

My eyes drift down the woman's slim figure, drinking in the shimmering silver gown that hugs her curves like it was painted on her perfect body. She spins around, and I suck in a breath at the sight of her bare back. Her dress plunges down to reveal her spine, a single twinkling strand of crystals holding the two sides of her dress together.

Curling my fingers into a fist, I let my tongue drag over my lips. My mouth is dry. I watch the woman take a flute of champagne with a nod, drinking it down in only a few gulps. She turns to listen to an older woman speak.

I want to feel her silken skin beneath my fingers. I want to bury my head in her soft black hair and inhale her scent. I want to drag my tongue over every inch of her skin and reveal all the secrets that dress is hiding.

I try to look away, but my body feels alive for the first time in years. Heat curls in my core at the sight of her leaning toward her mother, the long column of her neck exposed.

I'm not here to meet anyone. I'm only here to say congratulations to the monarchs and then slip out without anyone noticing. The King and I have become closer since he took the throne, as he's trying to rid Farcliff Court of all the corrupt, venomous courtiers his father supported. Ever since my brother died, I've wanted to do the same.

But tonight isn't about business. It's about congratulating the royal family and making an appearance, then leaving before it gets so torturous I want to follow my brother to the grave.

Flicking my eyes to the opposite corner of the room, my mouth tastes bitter. I pinch my lips together as I watch that snake, Gregory, pretend to laugh at someone's joke.

I can't be in the same room as him. I can't watch him swan around the room like he doesn't belong in jail. Every time I see his name in the papers, extolling his virtues and congratulating him on his donations to medical research, it makes me want to wreck something. Or someone. Mostly him.

The Count lifts his eyes, and my blood turns to ice. He's seen her. His lips have tugged into a horrid smile, and I watch his hand drift unconsciously toward his waistband.

Disgusting. He wouldn't be worthy of kissing her shoes, let alone touching himself at the sight of her.

I glance at the woman again, feeling a tug in the center of my chest. Her mother—at least, I assume it's her mother, based on how similar they look—grabs her elbow and whispers something in her ear. They start walking. Count Gregory watches my girl's every move, and I realize she's heading toward him.

No.

Fuck no.

No fucking way.

Anger bubbles through my veins. Everything's hot. I tug the collar of my shirt, wishing I hadn't tied my bowtie quite so tight.

Then, as if she senses me, she lifts her eyes to mine. I'm nailed to this spot on the floor. I can't move. For the few seconds that she keeps her eyes on mine, the pain inside me dulls ever so slightly. Ever since my family died, there's been a high-pitched humming in my ears. It quiets down, and I almost feel like myself again.

God, I want to touch her. I need to know what she tastes like. I need to wrap my arms around her and hold her close.

But she drags her eyes away from mine and paints a smile on those perfect lips, the guests parting to let her pass as she walks straight to Count fucking Gregory.

4

ADA

EVERY CELL in my body is tuned into the Duke of Blythe's frequency. Even from across the room, his eyes are magnetic. I can't see the color of them, but I can imagine the shifting green within them. My heart thumps as my whole body heats, caught somewhere between walking and stumbling as my parents drag me across the room.

Reluctantly, I look away from the Duke to make sure I don't fall flat on my face. I'm breathless.

Stealing a glance across the room, disappointment crashes into me when I see he's gone. The space he only just occupied is empty, and I feel an ache in the center of my chest.

Silly. That's all I am. I had a glass of champagne on an empty stomach and I'm already a little tipsy. That's the only explanation for my light-headedness and the feeling that my tongue is made of lead.

My mother comes to a stop, giving a warm greeting to Count Gregory.

His thin lips curl into a cold smile, and he drops them to

touch my mother's extended fingers. "Duchess Belcourt," he croons, smiling as his eyes remain dark. "Ravishing as always." He greets my father, then, and finally turns to me.

The warmth that ran down my spine when the Duke of Blythe looked at me evaporates. In its place, a slimy, cold feeling inches over my skin, crawling across my pores. I shiver.

"Good evening, Lady Belcourt. I was saddened to hear about your sister's accident, but I'm so very glad you were able to take her place."

His lips curl up farther, but I wouldn't quite call it a smile. With a hawk nose and dark eyes, the Count looks more dangerous than friendly. He extends his hand toward me, and I slip my fingers against his, fighting the urge to shudder.

When his lips touch my fingers, I want to puke.

My sister can't marry this man.

No way.

No, no, no.

Panic swells inside me as the Count straightens, his eyes dropping from my face down the length of my body. That slimy, cold feeling follows his gaze. I don't care how rich he is, how well-connected and well-titled he is. He shouldn't be looking at anyone like that when he's promised to my sister. Especially not me.

His gaze lingers on my chest, and I suddenly hate the fact that this gown is backless. I'm not wearing a bra, and I feel so incredibly naked. Exposed. Oh, I wish I were wearing a thousand layers to cover myself up! My hands itch to cross over my chest, but I hold them straight at my sides, my clutch gripped against my thigh.

Sucking in a breath, I clear my throat. "Lovely to meet you," I lie. "Maggie tells me you enjoy hunting."

From the time I was a toddler until now, I've been trained to act like a lady. That's the only thing working right now. It's keeping my spine straight and my smile from slipping. It's helping me nod and smile and ask follow-up questions as the Count tells me of his hunting trips and many rifles.

Panic trills inside me as my breath grows shallower.

I don't like this man. I can't let Maggie marry him. We'll figure something else out. We'll find another husband for her, or me. Kiera can get a scholarship. A loan.

Anything but him. Not Count Gregory.

A trumpet sounds, and everyone in the room hushes at once. We all turn toward the entrance as an expectant whisper ripples through the audience.

The King, Queen, and newborn Prince are arriving.

A sick feeling still churns in my gut, but I shove it aside. My eyes drift over the audience, searching for the Duke of Blythe. Maybe the sight of him will steady me. But as I scan the crowd in the ballroom, I can't see him anywhere.

All the guests in the room are being ushered into a long line across the room, presumably so the King and Queen can greet us all one by one. I make sure to put as much distance between me and the Count as possible, even though my mother gives me a disapproving glance.

Can she not sense the predatory energy he's giving off? Does she not have alarm bells ringing in her head from his nearness?

Closing my eyes, I take a spot next to my father. That puts both my mother and father between me and the Count, but it's still not enough. Nervous energy ripples through the guests as the King and Queen approach, their steps echoing in the long hallway leading to the ballroom.

That's not why I'm nervous, though. My cheeks feel red.

My heart is hammering. My mouth tastes of metal, and I wish I could get out of here.

"I never liked Count Gregory," a male voice says in my ear. "I don't blame you for that reaction."

His voice sounds like warm honey with a hint of spice. Gravel rattles around at the edges, with the depth and resonance that screams *male*.

I open my eyes, but I already know who it is. The Duke of Blythe stares back at me, his face mere inches from mine.

The pictures didn't do him justice.

A thousand shades of green with little speckles of gold. A fine, long nose and regal brow. When my eyes drop to his lips, my breath catches. Full and pink, they make me want to lean in and feel them against my own.

"Your Grace," I stammer, racking my brain for the correct title. Is it Your Grace? Or just Lord Blythe? Sir? Mister? Suddenly, my training doesn't seem so foolproof.

"You're blushing." His eyebrow arches as a smile quirks his lips.

I blush harder, which makes his lips tug even more.

"Aren't you going to tell me your name?"

God, if I could bottle his voice up and sell it, I'd make millions. It sends little thrills rushing through my veins, warming me up from top to bottom. I'd swoon to him reading me a recipe book.

"Ada," I answer simply.

Before he can say anything, all attention turns to the entrance. The King and Queen have arrived. The King is dressed in his ceremonial uniform, with a gold crown nestled in his hair. His broad, muscular shoulders taper down to a thin waist, and he keeps one hand on his queen's lower back.

Queen Elle was a commoner not long ago, but you'd never guess it now. Dressed in an emerald gown with a sparkling tiara in her short, dark hair, she looks as regal as any regent who went before her. A member of staff whispers names of attendees to her before she greets them, smiling warmly at each and every person.

In her arms, her first child sleeps soundly. The three of them—the King, Queen, and their heir—make such a perfect image, it makes my heart ache. I can almost feel the love radiating between them.

My sister will never have that. Will I? Or will I be married off to some rich old man who can elevate our family's standing?

Her Majesty the Queen greets Count Gregory, and my mouth sours. My sister won't get everlasting love like the Queen has. Not if she has to marry the Count.

I stiffen as I watch the older man give a deep bow to the monarchs, unable to hide my aversion.

Then, a warm hand slides over my lower back. "Try not to make your distaste so obvious, Ada," the Duke whispers in my ear. "If everyone knows exactly how you feel about them, you'll make lots of enemies around here."

He takes his hand away, but not before my whole core blazes. I can feel the imprint of his hand on my lower back, and the spot where his thumb just brushed against my exposed skin. Heat rises up my neck.

Don't look at him. Don't look at him. Don't look at him.

I look at the Duke, but I should have listened to myself and resisted the urge. His eyes bore into mine, and heat whips through my body like a fire through a field of dry grasses. It carves a wide path down my spine, making every part of my body burn hotter. My nipples pebble against the silver fabric of my dress, and I suck my lip between my teeth, drawing the Duke's gaze.

His eyes darken at the sight of my mouth, and the heat in

my core cranks higher. A man has never looked at me like *that* before. Like he lives to look at me. Like he wants to eat me.

"Lady Belcourt," the Queen says, and I snap my head back to meet her gaze. Standing before me, she's at least six inches taller than me. She used to be a rower at Farcliff University, apparently. An athlete.

I mumble a greeting and sink down in a curtsy, dropping my head as I rise again.

"I saw you at the Farcliff Jubilee Concert Hall last month," the Queen says. "You played beautifully."

"You...you were there? And you saw me playing?" My father stiffens beside me, and I know I'm messing this up. I gulp. "I mean, thank you, Your Majesty."

The Queen smiles just as her child blinks awake. He makes a soft noise, spittle bubbling at his lips. The Queen's eyes soften as her son reaches for her. The baby turns his head to me and giggles, reaching a tiny, closed fist in my direction.

"I think baby Charlie likes you." The Queen laughs, and the King leans over to chuck his son's cheek.

The King meets my eyes. "We're looking forward to coming to your Christmas concert in three weeks' time." He smiles at me, as if he isn't the literal King of Farcliff.

They're looking forward to *my* concert? What?

I dip into another curtsy, and the Queen moves over to speak to the Duke. Vaguely, I notice that the King seems very familiar with the Duke, and even shakes his hand and calls the Duke by his first name. *Heath.* Yum.

When the monarchs move on to the next guest, I steal a glance at the Duke of Blythe. He meets my gaze, his eyes impossible to read. It's not until the greetings are over and the

King and Queen announce the official start of the ball that I remember to take a full breath again.

By the time I come back to myself, the Duke has disappeared from my side.

5

ADA

MY HEAD IS A MESS. Count Gregory keeps asking me questions, and my parents keep staring at me like my brain is leaking out of my ears. I can't seem to make sentences. My body is still on fire, and my eyes search everywhere for the Duke. I need to get away from all these people.

I ignore my mother's disproving stare and drink another glass of champagne. It only makes me feel worse. My stomach churns as the alcohol hits it, and...oh, shit. I shouldn't have drunk that so quickly. My mouth fills with saliva, and I have that horrible sensation rising in my throat...

No, no, no.

Stumbling to the bathroom, I throw open a stall door and puke into a toilet. As my eyes water and I spit bile into the bowl, I realize the toilet is inlaid with gold buttons to flush. Lovely. What a nice touch. Only the best for a duchess to hurl into.

When I exit the stall, the restroom attendant directs me to the vanity and lays a brand-new toothbrush and travel-sized toothpaste next to the sink. I pinch my lips into a smile and thank her, embarrassment ripping through my chest.

Once I've cleaned myself up and my mouth is minty-fresh, I find a sofa in the corner—yes, in the bathroom—and pull out my phone. I need a minute.

Ada: Saw the Duke. No selfie yet.

Kiera sees the message, three dots appearing on the screen within an instant.

Kiera: GET TO WORK.

Smiling, I let my shoulders relax. Pulling out a compact to touch up my makeup, I take a deep breath and steel myself for the crowd outside.

It's not that crowds make me uncomfortable, exactly. It's just that I feel like I don't belong here. Sure, my family has royal lineage. We have lands and titles and an official royal invitation to the Christmas Ball.

But my gown is rented. I don't have sapphires dripping down my neck, and I only know the names of most people here because I've studied pictures of them. Just like the staff.

But the worst part is that every time Count Gregory speaks, his eyes snaking down my body in a way that makes me feel ill, all I can do is think of my sister.

She's marrying him.

The beautiful, elegant ballerina is marrying a creepy old Count who can't keep his eyes to himself.

It just... It makes me feel sick. Clearly.

The restroom door opens, and my childhood best friend walks through. Rhoda is tall and graceful, with hair like spun gold. She's wearing a cobalt gown that makes her deep-blue eyes sparkle.

"Ada." She smiles, spreading her arms. "I saw you rushing in here a few minutes ago. How are you?"

"I'm okay," I answer, standing up to give my friend a quick squeeze. I haven't seen Rhoda in about a year. Ever since we graduated from college, we've tried to stay in touch—but life tends to get in the way. We've drifted apart.

I pull away, shaking my head. "You look amazing."

"Got rid of my dorky aesthetic once I graduated college," she laughs, tucking a strand of hair behind her ear. A massive diamond engagement ring glitters on her finger. Wait... Rhoda's *engaged*?

I gasp. "Rhoda!"

"Oh, this?" She looks at her finger, smiling.

"Who is he?"

She holds out her hand as I lean over her ring, watching how the light catches every facet cut into the stone. When I look up, Rhoda smiles. "It's the Duke of Harbor. We're having an engagement party next week. You should have received the invitation already."

"The Duke of Harbor?" I frown, pulling away. "He's nearly seventy years old."

"Ain't nothin' but a number," she says, laughing, but the light doesn't quite reach her eyes. "Sixty-two," she adds. "Hardly *almost seventy*."

My chest clenches. A lump grows in my throat. It hurts to swallow past it. "Congratulations."

Rhoda gives me a tight smile, nodding. "Thank you. It's a good match. My family is pleased."

A good match.

I nod. "And you?"

"Me, what?"

"Are you pleased?" I ask, tilting my head.

Rhoda's cheeks grow red and she ducks her head to the side, pulling out a bullet of lipstick from her clutch. "He's kind to me. And he cares about animals."

"Will you be able to finish your PhD? He's from another

generation, Rhoda. He might not approve of you staying in school after the marriage."

Rhoda shrugs. "He'll have to. I only have a year left before I defend my thesis."

Forcing a smile, I sling my arm around Rhoda's waist. "I'm happy for you," I lie.

The truth is, I'm not happy for her. I feel sick. She's just like my sister—marrying an older man just to make her family happy. Is this what our world has come to? Court life dictates a lot of our actions, but we're not living in the Middle Ages. I thought we'd moved past arranged marriages and *good matches*.

Swallowing down bile—I will *not* throw up again—I fluff my hair in the mirror. "My sister's supposed to marry Count Gregory."

Rhoda's hand pauses, the lipstick hovering near her lips. Her eyes meet mine in the mirror, and a veil of sadness covers her face. "Oh."

I pinch a bitter smile. "Yeah."

"He's..." She shakes her head. "I've heard rumors about his temper."

"But he's rich and well-titled, and the Belcourts are on the decline. Kiera needs to get into a good college, and Gregory has all the connections. It's a good match." I can't keep the revulsion out of my voice, and Rhoda drops her lipstick.

She wraps her arms around me, squeezing tight. "It'll be okay. The Count donates to all major universities on the continent. Doesn't he spend half his earnings on medical research? That's a sign of someone who cares."

"Or a sign of someone who has vested interest in a particular industry." I sigh, shaking my head. "I don't even know what I'm saying. He could be a saint for all I know. I just don't like the way he looks at me." I glance at Rhoda, forcing a smile. "At least the Duke of Harbor is handsome in a silver fox kind of way."

Rhoda laughs, nodding. "I think I can grow to love him."

Sadness bubbles up in my chest, pressing against my ribs until they nearly crack from the pressure. I've been living a fantasy, thinking I could marry who I pleased and live the life I want. I believed my sisters and I could choose our partners and carve our own way in the world.

But between Maggie and Rhoda, I'm starting to realize that's not true. How long will it be until a match is found for me? How old will I be when my parents decide I need to marry?

The King is my second cousin. I'm not a nobody, and marrying badly would bring shame on my family, no matter who Maggie ends up with.

As Rhoda finishes touching up her makeup, her big diamond ring glittering on her finger, I can see my future. She's my future. Maggie is my future.

I'm not living my own life. I may be a concert pianist, earning the praise of the Queen. I may be wearing a pretty dress and attending the Christmas Ball at Farcliff Castle. I may be smiling and drinking champagne, but I'm on borrowed time.

Soon a husband will be chosen for me, too, and I'll have to learn to love him, or tolerate him—or at the very least, accept him.

Painting a false smile on my face, I head for the door with Rhoda, pushing it open and steeling myself against the weight of diamonds and sapphires and expectations. They're all starting to feel more like shackles and chains than luxuries.

I shake my head, clearing the thought away.

I'm fortunate to have been born into this family. Not

many people get to come to the castle like this. My life is comfortable.

But comfort has a price, and I'm only just realizing I'm going to have to pay it sooner rather than later.

A shadow falls over my shoulders as Count Gregory appears by my side. He peers at me over his long hook nose, his eyes drifting down to my chest.

That slimy feeling inches down my spine, and I take half a step back to put some space between us.

"Would you do me the honor of a dance?" the Count asks, his thin lips curling upward.

Trying to quell the panic inside me, I give him a curt nod. "Of course."

When the Count's hand touches the crook of my lower back, I try not to flinch. If I hadn't just emptied my stomach, I'd want to do it now. I keep my lips mashed together and my face as relaxed as I can, but the woodenness of my steps almost betrays me.

Leading me to the center of the dance floor, the Count opens his arms with a flourish. "You look angelic, Lady Belcourt." He bares his teeth in a sorry excuse for a smile.

I drop into a curtsy just to avoid eye contact.

When my palm slides over his hand, a shiver passes through me. Bitter bile clings to my throat when the Count places his hand on my hip, but all my years of training help me keep a placid smile on my face. The musicians start playing a waltz, and the dance begins.

How long does one dance last?

An eternity.

I feel naked. Exposed. The Count's gaze is lecherous, his lips curled into a disgusting smirk.

He's marrying my sister, and he's looking at me like that. He's *marrying* my *sister*. I can't let that happen! But what can I do? It'll be announced within weeks, once Maggie's foot is healed enough for public appearances.

"I was disappointed to hear your sister wouldn't be attending tonight, but I could never have imagined the pleasure of your company," the Count says, dropping his voice to a low rasp. It grates on my skin like nails on a chalkboard.

I stare at a mole on his neck. At the two long, wiry hairs sticking out of it.

Gulping, I nod. "Thank you, Your Excellency."

"Call me Chester, please," he croons, leaning close to me. He smells like mothballs and stale red wine.

I squeeze my eyes shut, focusing on the movement of my feet.

"You move so gracefully," he starts again, clearly trying to get more of a response out of me. "I would have guessed you're the ballerina in the family."

That earns a barking laugh from me. My dancing is stilted, to say the least. I can play music, of course. I can let go and feel the rhythm when I'm sitting in front of a piano.

But dancing? Using my body to convey emotion?

I'm hopeless.

"Seeing you here almost makes me feel like I've chosen the wrong Lady Belcourt," Count Gregory says, his voice nothing more than a whisper. His words slither over my skin, making my eyes snap open.

My head spins. I trip over my feet, stepping the wrong way as the Count tries to lead me over the dance floor. I can't hear the music anymore because my heartbeat is rushing so hard.

I need to get away. Run, run, *run*.

Every instinct is screaming at me. Every muscle wound tight. Every part of my brain blaring *danger*!

There's fight and flight—but I just freeze. My body keeps

moving mechanically as the waltz continues, led by the Count as we circle around the dance floor. I can't pull away. I can't push him off me. It's like everything inside me just stops working while my mind runs into overdrive.

"May I cut in?" A warm voice slices through the panic in my mind.

The Duke.

Count Gregory's face falls, pure hatred shining in his eyes. I notice the waltz has ended and a space has opened up around me, the Duke, and Count Gregory. People are watching.

How could they not?

The Duke of Blythe doesn't attend balls. When he does, he sits in a corner and disappears after an hour.

He doesn't dance.

But—

"Of course," Count Gregory says, clenching his jaw so tight I think I hear a crack. When he takes a step away from me, I let out a breath.

The Duke turns to face me, ignoring the murderous look in Count Gregory's eyes. He looks at me, his eyes like shards of green glass. Holding out a hand, he waits for me to step to him.

Even that tiny moment—waiting for me to come to him, giving me control over how he touches my body, asking for my permission—I notice. It means something to me. It makes the tightness in my body ease ever so slightly.

I lift my arm up to his shoulder as a quiet murmur goes through the guests, but I can't look away from his face. "You're dancing," I say, my mouth still stiff and full of cotton balls.

"Not quite yet," the Duke grins, those full lips tugging up at the edge.

Slowly, the discomfort ebbs away from my body. My veins

shake off some of the icicles that had started growing in them, and a soft warmth grows in the pit of my stomach.

The music starts. Another waltz.

This time, I don't feel wooden and mechanical. I stare at the Duke's face, letting out a long breath as the safety of his arms starts to loosen me up.

"Thank you," I finally manage to say, shaking my head. "That was uncomfortable. You saved me."

The Duke grins. "Are you sure I'm any better?"

There's danger in his eyes. Not the way Count Gregory's eyes spoke danger. The Duke's gaze doesn't make a shot of cold jet down my spine. The opposite happens. Fire roars in the pit of my stomach, sending spears of heat down my thighs.

"Yes," I answer. "You are."

"What if I'm worse than he is? A wolf in sheep's clothing."

"A wolf in a well-tailored tux."

That earns me a laugh, and oh, I want to make him laugh again. I want to see the way his eyes crinkle. How dimples appear in his cheeks. How his lips stretch over his perfect, white teeth, and the sound of his warm laughter sends another shot of heat straight through my chest.

He sweeps me around the dance floor, and I vaguely realize that most people have stepped off to watch us. The Duke's eyes are trained on mine, his hand splaying over my mid-back. Skin on skin. Supporting me. Marking me. Making heat spill over my body in waves.

"I didn't know you attended this type of event."

"I don't," he answers. "But it's the young Prince Charles' first Christmas, and it would be frowned upon to miss it. Even for me." He grins, and another wave of heat crashes over my thighs.

How is it possible for one smile to have that effect on me?

It's like he knows a secret, and he's only sharing it with me. It makes my pulse quicken as every inch of my body grows more sensitive. I can feel every finger of his hand on my back. The way his index finger is curled slightly, pressing into my flesh. The way his sleeve brushes against my wrist where our hands are clasped. How the lapel of his jacket feels beneath the fingertips of my other hand.

"What have you heard about me?" the Duke asks, but I have a feeling he doesn't care about the answer. His eyes drop to my lips, as if he's only asking something to hear me speak.

"I heard you have women brought to your estate," I blurt out, immediately feeling a rush of heat and blood blooming over my cheeks.

His eyebrow twitches as mirth sparkles in his eyes. "Oh?"

I shake my head. "I'm sorry. I shouldn't—"

"Don't apologize." The Duke's voice drops, sending another thrill coursing through my veins. He pulls me closer, and I catch a whiff of his scent. Strong, heady, spicy. I close my eyes as every cell in my body tightens in anticipation. I wonder if he can see my nipples tightening beneath my dress.

Would I mind if he could? The thought of him seeing my arousal makes my body wind tighter.

"Do you like the thought of women being delivered to my bed?" he asks, not trying to hide the humor in his words.

"No," I answer, blushing harder.

"Why not?"

I don't answer. Instead, I just stare into his emerald eyes. They shine brighter than any gemstone in the room. Complicated, unreadable, and totally focused on me.

The music ends, and the Duke drops his hand from my back. He lifts the other hand up, still clasped in mine, and gives the audience a bow. Everyone is staring. Clapping. Whispering to each other behind raised hands.

Count Gregory is there, arms crossed, looking homicidal.

I glance away, squeezing the Duke's fingers so hard he winces.

Hooking my hand in the crook of his elbow, he leans into my ear. "Come with me. I want to show you something."

Everyone is watching. I shouldn't follow him. I should excuse myself and find Rhoda, or my parents, or someone more acceptable to speak to.

But my body doesn't cooperate. I let the Duke lead me across the room as guests part for us like a school of fish around a shark. I can feel their eyes, but the heat of their stares pales in comparison to the fire the Duke has lit inside me.

6

HEATH

COUNT GREGORY'S eyes burn holes through the side of my head, and I love every second of it.

Watch me walk away with the woman you're drooling over. Watch me destroy everything you like, just like you did to me. In a few short weeks, watch me destroy everything you hold dear. Your fortune. Your reputation. Your life.

Hatred burns hot, but there's something else. Something that wells up from a deeper place, behind the anger and the pain and the loathing.

Why did I feel the need to cut in between the Count and Ada dancing? Why did the sight of them together make me feel like shoving a knife straight through his heart?

As I slide my hand over Ada's back, feeling the silkiness of her skin beneath my palm, a sense of calm washes over me.

It's her. Ada Belcourt.

Maybe I like the way her mouth turned down when Gregory kissed her fingers. Maybe I enjoyed watching her grow stiff when he led her to the dance floor. Her obvious dislike for him makes me feel like I've found someone who gets it. Someone who sees past the wealth and the titles. Who sees the monster he really is.

But as I glance at her, watching the pulse thump through her neck, there's something more. Her body is so reactive to me. So pliable. So incredibly irresistible.

I don't like her because she obviously dislikes the Count. She's awoken something inside me that I thought died a long time ago. She makes heat burn through my core. I'm already addicted to her presence.

I hate Christmas. It reminds me of death. I haven't celebrated it in four years, and this year wasn't supposed to be any different. Attending the Christmas Ball was a show of support for the King and Queen, who have always been kind to me. It was a message to the King that I'm on his side. Nothing more.

I'm not supposed to stay here tonight. I'm supposed to leave right after the royal greetings, which have already happened. My lawyers have warned me against spending any time with the Count. There's too much at stake.

I definitely shouldn't be stepping in between him and a woman he's interested in.

But I just...don't care. Can't stop myself. Need to be near her.

My pants are tight and my blood is running hot, and I want to be alone with her. I want to watch her tuck her hair behind her ear and reward me with a shy smile.

I want a lot more, too, but I'm not sure I deserve it.

7

ADA

"WHERE ARE YOU TAKING ME?" My voice is low.

"Away from prying eyes," the Duke answers.

A thrill shoots down my spine, settling deep in my womb. I clench against the emptiness between my legs, letting my eyelids flutter closed for a moment.

Does he have any idea what his voice does to me? How his hand on my back makes my head spin? How for the first time since college, I feel like more than just a person—I feel like a woman who wants and needs and craves?

We walk for what feels like a long time, but it's probably only a few minutes. The sounds of the ball fade in the distance as our footsteps echo in the hallway.

"Here," the Duke says, his voice low. He pushes a heavy wooden door open for me, and I step through, taking a moment for my eyes to adjust to the darkness.

We're in a medium-sized room with tall, floor-to-ceiling windows overlooking Farcliff Lake. The night sky is dark, with a big, yellow moon hanging low in the sky. In front of the windows is a grand piano, gleaming bronze with the light of the moon.

I gasp, recognizing the piano even in the darkness. It's the custom-made Blythe grand piano, made for the previous royals.

This piano is a thing of legends. King Charlie's mother used to play, and it's rumored this piano cost over two million dollars to make. I walk up to the instrument, almost afraid to touch it. Different types of wood are inlaid so perfectly that the instrument looks like a watercolor painting. I run my fingers over the polished wood, eyes wide and heart thumping.

"You should play it," the Duke says, stripping his tuxedo jacket off and laying it over the arm of a sofa. His white shirt stretches over his chest and arms, betraying the raw power of the muscles coiled underneath it. His broad shoulders taper to slim hips, and I wonder if there's a deep V carved between his hips.

My cheeks burn. I shake my head, gulping. "I couldn't."

"Why not?" He settles onto the couch, letting his arm hang over the back of the leather sofa. His other elbow rests on his jacket, his head propped between his thumb and index finger. He watches me, eyes hanging low.

I stand next to the piano, letting my hand drift to the cover protecting the keys. I shake my head. "It's not mine to play."

"No one's touched it in years. Not since the Queen Mother died. Instruments are meant to be played."

I glance at the Duke. He looks completely at ease here, his ankle resting on his opposite knee. Head still propped in his fingers. Arm slung over the back of the sofa.

How did he even know this piano was here?

"Ada," he says, and a shiver tumbles through my veins. *Say it again, please. Say my name.* I glance at him, eyes widening. He nods to the instrument. "Play for me."

The command sends a thrill rushing through my body. My body clenches, skin too sensitive against the silky material of my gown.

"What do you want me to play?" My voice is a breath. A whisper.

"Something sad," the Duke replies. "Anything but Christmas music."

I glance at the man on the sofa, remembering that it was right before Christmas when his brother was found. The anniversary of his death will be coming up next week, or the one after. I'm not sure of the exact date.

Moonlight cuts across his angular features, casting half his face in darkness. He holds my gaze, and for just a moment I see pain flash across his eyes.

He lost his whole family four years ago. He's been carrying the dukedom on his shoulders since then. Everyone thinks he's a recluse who has women and booze delivered to his door—but for just a moment, I see him. The real him. The man who's been cut deep, who's been suffering on his own. The man who has taken the responsibility for his lands, and by all accounts let the family business die.

Is that true, though?

How did he know where this piano was? I saw the familiar way King Charlie spoke to him. Like they're friends. He's probably at the castle all the time.

Then his face grows stone-hard, and his expression is shuttered again.

I swallow past a thorny mess in my throat and sit down at the piano bench, lifting the cover to reveal the black and white keys. My fingers drift over them. Smooth and polished and familiar.

I'm glad the couch is behind me; I wouldn't be able to play if I could see the Duke in my peripheral vision. Even the prickling of his gaze on my bare back makes all my senses heighten.

I close my eyes and try to forget he's here. Kicking my heels off, I feel the rightmost pedal under my foot. Then, with a breath, I start to play.

I've always loved Chopin. His nocturnes are full of tragedy and complicated emotions, pierced with positive moments that dissolve into nothing. For the Duke, I play my favorite one. Number 19, Opus 72, in E minor.

Playing one of my favorite pieces of music on the royal grand piano worth almost as much as my entire family's estate sends me somewhere deep. I forget where I am. Who I'm with. Why I'm here.

It's just me and the music, until I sense the Duke get up. He comes to stand beside the piano, watching my fingers dance over the keys. His presence only intensifies the moment. He breathes in the melody, staring at me. Feeling me.

My whole body grows electric. My breasts feel heavy. Arms feel light. A bud of heat unfurls in the pit of my stomach as the Duke listens to me play. His grip on the edge of the piano tightens as his breath grows shorter. I can almost feel it whisper over my skin, but I keep playing.

A strand of hair falls across my face. I ignore it.

It's not until the music ends that I take my hands off the keys, place them in my lap, and I take a full breath. I lift my eyes to the Duke, almost afraid of what I'll find.

His face is cracked open, pain and desire and wonder carved into every feature. Every curve of his lips. Every eyelash and indescribable shade of green.

"Stand up," he rasps.

I stand.

He reaches for me, circling his arm around my waist and

tugging me close. I crash against his chest, catching myself against the fine white fabric of his shirt. My eyes widen, head spinning from the closeness of him.

"I want to kiss you," he says, his voice strained. His eyes angle toward me, dropping to my lips. His brows draw closer, as if he's in immense pain. "Tell me I can kiss you."

My voice catches. Breath stays stuck somewhere in my throat as my body screams at me to comply. As my fingers curl around the nape of his neck, feeling the softness of his dark hair, I finally part my lips.

"You can kiss me," I whisper.

I expect him to crush his lips against mine. To make the inferno inside me burn hotter. To cut me open and watch me bleed out.

But he hesitates, lifting his eyes to mine. "Ada," he rasps. "Tell me you want me to."

My heart thumps so hard I know he can feel it. My breasts are pressed against the thin fabric of his shirt, my nipples sensitive buds against his chest. My core is burning so hot I wonder if he can sense it. If he knows how wet it is between my legs. If he understands that never have I ever felt like this before. Never have I ever wanted this as badly as I do now.

"Kiss me, Your Grace. Please." Am I begging? Is that pathetic?

I don't care.

His arms are around my waist and his chest is pressed against mine. It smells like him everywhere. I'm breathing him in. I can feel the pulse hammering through his body, and something hard throbs between his legs.

He lets out a low groan, closing his eyes. His hold on me doesn't loosen. Instead, his hand sweeps up my side, brushing my waist and teasing the edge of my breast. When his fingers slide over my jaw, his thumb brushing over the gloss on my lips, he shakes his head.

"The moment you walked into that ballroom, I knew you'd be mine tonight."

His eyes are dark. Hungry.

My body begs for him. I cling to him, not caring that my nails are digging into the nape of his neck.

And the Duke listens. He angles his mouth to mine and kisses me, his lips parting as a soft groan slips through them.

I melt. Burn. Need.

My arms circle his neck as he deepens our kiss, his hand still cupping my cheek as his other arm slides down to rest against the dimples on my lower back. He presses me against his body, grinding his hips toward me.

He's hard.

Oh my God, he's hard. For me. Right now. At the royal ball.

His tongue slides over my bottom lip and then dips inside my mouth, and I taste him for the first time. Hot and spicy and so deliciously male. My whole body thrums for him as he backs me against the side of the piano, his hands sweeping down to my waist to hold me in place.

"I'd fuck you right here against that piano," he groans, nipping at my bottom lip. Kissing my jaw, my neck, my earlobe.

Dirty, dirty Duke.

How did I get here again? Do I even care?

I pant, clinging to his broad shoulders. "That's where I draw the line," I say, leaning my head back as he kisses the space between my breasts. His hands cup them, squeezing gently as he runs his thumb over the fabric of my gown, feeling the pebbled nipples that have been hard for him all night.

"You won't fuck me?" He lifts his head to glance at me, his lips tugged into a smirk. As if it's a challenge. As if he can make me change my mind.

"I won't desecrate this piano that way," I say, fire burning deep in my core. I know my eyes are full of desire. I know he sees the way he's unravelling me with little more than a kiss.

I don't care.

All the tension inside me needs release. All the stress of the evening needs an escape.

And damn it, he's perfect. He's broad and strong and commanding, and he makes my panties so wet they cling to me.

I can have one night, can't I? Soon, I'll be like Maggie or Rhoda. I'll have someone chosen for me. I'll have to marry for honor or titles. I'll have my whole life laid out for me, and I won't be able to do this. It could be my last chance. My one night of passion.

Why not with the Duke of Blythe?

The chances of seeing him again are slim. He's a recluse. I won't run into him at the concert hall. If things get awkward, it'll only be for tonight.

And his lips are firm, yet soft. His hands are broad with long, fine fingers that make my pulse thump. And he's hard. For me. Right now.

The Duke lets out a low rumble. It rattles through my chest as he stands tall, pressing his body against mine. The cold, polished wood of the piano is behind me, and the Duke's hot body in front. I lift my eyes to his, loving the way he sinks his fingers into my hips.

"For the record," he says with a grin, "I don't have women delivered to the estate."

"No?"

He shakes his head, moving his fingers to the zipper at the

side of my dress. "I haven't made love to a woman in two years."

The teeth of the zipper catch as he tugs, slowly lowering it down as my pulse quickens.

"No?" I repeat, breathless.

He shakes his head.

"Why not?"

One big boulder of a shoulder moves up in half a shrug as his hand keeps moving my zipper down. "Didn't fill the void inside me. Made me feel emptier. So I stopped."

"And tonight? Me?"

He doesn't answer. The zipper is undone, and the Duke moves his hands to my shoulders. He slides the silver fabric over my skin, letting it puddle at my feet.

Apart from a tiny thong covering the space between my legs, I'm naked. He's not.

His eyes darken, drinking in every inch of my body. The backs of his fingers touch my bare stomach, sending a tremor straight through my core. He runs his hand higher up, turning it around to sweep his palm over the top of my breast. His thumb teases my nipple.

I shiver, but not from the cold.

Finally, the Duke speaks. His voice is low. His eyes dark. "Tonight," he says, "you're mine."

8

ADA

Reaching for the Duke's bowtie, I unfasten it with long, slow movements. He watches, standing before me unmoving.

"If anyone were to walk in right now..."

"They won't," he answers, completely sure of himself.

I bite my lip, eliciting a groan from the Duke. I tug his bowtie free and lay it gently against the piano bench, then move to his shirt. Before my hands can get there, though, the Duke is unbuttoning it.

I don't know what it is about the sight of him tugging those little white buttons open, but it sends heat ripping through my core. The broad palms. The tendons and muscles flexing over the back of his hand. The sliver of exposed chest growing wider, and wider, and wider.

When he pulls the shirt free from his pants, I suck in a hard breath.

There's a V, and it's glorious. Carved deep into his abdominal muscles, it leads my eyes down to the promise of something good. Crawling my gaze back up, I inhale every hard plane and sweeping muscle in front of me.

The Duke is more than a man. He's some sort of higher

being, crafted from stuff that isn't quite human. No one can be this perfect. It's not fair to other men. It's not fair to my poor, ruined panties.

Reaching for his chest, I let my fingers hover an inch from his skin. Flicking my eyes up to his, I see him grin.

"You can touch. I won't bite. Unless you want me to."

A blush creeps over my cheeks, my fingers still hovering close enough to feel the heat of his skin, but not close enough to touch. He catches them in his hand, bringing the tips of my fingers up to his mouth. A soft kiss lands on each fingertip, and my knees knock together. I feel weak.

His eyes drink me in. They're so green and deep with the pupils blown out, and I feel so incredibly naked and so incredibly good.

Then, the Duke parts his lips and takes the tips of my fingers in his mouth.

I melt. A breath escapes through my parted lips as my eyelids flutter, hardly able to take the closeness of someone who looks like sex incarnate. "Your Grace..."

"Heath," he says. "Call me Heath."

"Heath," I repeat in a whisper, knowing from my little sister's ramblings that he never lets anyone call him by his name. A thrill pierces my gut as the Duke—Heath—opens my palm and lays a soft kiss in the center of it.

With one step toward me, his chest brushes mine. I lean in, feeling the softness of my breasts press against the hardness of his muscle, tilting my head toward him.

I need more. I need his kiss. His hands. His cock.

I need everything he's willing to give me.

This could be the last time I feel this way. The only time! It could be my one chance with a man like him, who makes me feel like the world falls away. Who convinces me to play the royal piano and then undresses me beside it. Who takes my fingers in his mouth and seems to like the taste of my skin.

When Heath's hands slide over my hips, the warmth of his skin makes my breath catch. He drops his head to my neck, laying a kiss on my burning flesh.

I tilt my head to the side, closing my eyes.

My head spins. It's too much. Not enough.

My own hands run up every ridge and valley of his muscles, committing them all to memory. I want to be able to call up the sight of his body whenever I need it. I want to remember every taste. Every smell. Every touch. I want to remember the way my heart skips a beat whenever a soft groan slips through his lips. How a touch from his palm makes sparks explode across my skin.

Sliding his hands to my back, I feel him notch his thumbs into the dimples above my ass. They fit perfectly, like they were made for him. His hands slide over my ass, squeezing gently as he pulls me into him.

And I feel him. His tuxedo trousers do nothing to hide the bulge growing between his strong thighs. As the Duke kisses my neck, my shoulder, my jaw, I reach down to palm his stiffening cock.

He groans, and I revel in the noise.

I'm making him feel this way. I'm the reason he's making those noises. I'm the one who has him harder than steel. Is his cock weeping already, I wonder? Soaking into the fabric of his underwear? Throbbing every time I press my lips against his skin?

I wrap my fingers around his cock, wishing there were no fabric between us.

The Duke groans. He pulls his head away from my neck, staring into my eyes. "If you keep doing that, I'll come in my pants."

A wicked smile tugs·at my lips, and the Duke's eyes darken. He likes when I'm bad.

I give his cock another stroke, letting my lips part. Heath stares at my face, his eyelids dropping as my hand moves. Up and down. Up and down. The feeling of his hard cock makes all kinds of pressure build in the pit of my stomach.

Then, with a roar, the Duke pulls my hand away. He wraps his arms around me and throws me over his shoulder as if I weighed nothing, marching to the couch. He throws me down so I bounce on the soft cushions, catching myself before I tumble off. The Duke kneels before me, spreading my legs wide.

"Are you wet for me?" Heath asks, staring up at me through thick, black lashes. He pulls my legs so my ass is hanging off the edge of the sofa, then presses the inside of my knees wide until they're pinned against the soft leather.

My chest heaves. I bite my lip, unable to answer. His head is so close to my core he must be able to see the wetness soaking through my thong. He must be able to smell the arousal leaking out of me.

Using his big shoulder to keep my leg pinned against the sofa, the Duke slides his hand over the inside of my thigh and gently, oh so gently, tugs my panties over to the side. A satisfied groan reaches my ears, and I know he sees just how wet he's made me.

When I glance down at him, Heath has a smile on his lips. His thumb runs over the crook of my hip, so close to my outer lips. Not close enough. I sigh, leaning back against the sofa as he spreads me wide. Exposes me. Looks at me like no one has before.

"You're beautiful, Ada," he growls, letting his thumb tease just a bit closer to my weeping slit. His lips drop down to kiss the inside of my thigh, and my breath catches. That stubble tickles my skin, sending shivers of pleasure tumbling across my core.

With one hand pushing my knee wide and his shoulder pinning the other knee to the couch, I can't move. Not that I'd want to. The Duke has his head so close to my center, and all I want is to feel his tongue. His kiss. I want to feel those lush lips kissing me down there.

My cheeks are red and hot at the thought of it.

I'm not a virgin. I've fooled around with people. I dated a guy for three years when I was in college.

But never have I ever felt like this. Spread wide, exposed, begging for more.

"Please," I whisper, truly begging now. I don't care.

His thumb runs over my outer lip again, tugging gently to open me up. I gasp, my chest heaving as I try to regain control over my own body. I can feel the wetness seeping out of me, and I know he sees. He sees everything.

The Duke lays a soft kiss on the inside of my hip, then another, an inch closer. Another, closer again.

I can't breathe. I can't think. I need his lips right there where my body screams for him.

Hearing my unspoken pleas, the Duke complies. He spreads me wide with his hands. His tongue sweeps through my folds, tasting all of me.

I buck, but he holds me down. He laps up my desire with a low groan, and I nearly come apart. That noise. I want more of it. It's gruff, like his throat is full of gravel. So deliciously rough, and all for me.

His tongue moves slow, then fast. Soft, then hard. Teasing my bud, then moving lower. All the while, he holds me down against the sofa, his broad shoulders rounded between my legs, his head bowed as he devours me.

Tangling my fingers into his dark hair, I grind my center

into his face. The Duke hooks his arms around my legs, throwing them over his shoulders. I moan, clawing at the soft leather sofa to get some sort of leverage. To support my body as it's teased and torn apart.

With my legs over his shoulders, Heath runs his hands up to my waist, holding me down. His tongue slips down to my opening, and he drives it inside me.

I gasp. I fist my hand into his hair and pull as heat erupts in my core.

I've never had this before. Not like this. Not where I know —I just *know*—that Heath is enjoying it almost as much as I am. I can tell by the groans. The fingertips sinking into my flesh. The way his mouth eats me like I was made just for him.

And I come.

My orgasm erupts, sending daggers of heat down my thighs and out to every extremity. My back arches, and I clench. I'm so empty. So, so lacking. Even as my breath staggers and my orgasm crashes into me, making my cheeks pink and stealing my voice away, I know it's not enough.

The muscles in my core tighten and release, aching for something long and hard and male.

When I can breathe again, I lift my head and look at the Duke. That wolfish grin is on his lips again, glistening with my arousal.

"Did you enjoy that?" His voice is a low rumble, sending another thrill tickling down my spine. He runs his hands up my sides to tease the underside of my breast, his eyes sweeping down my body and back up again.

"Not bad," I answer, sucking my bottom lip between my teeth.

Heath grins, hooking his fingers in my ruined panties and

tugging them down my legs. I help him by kicking them off, not caring where they land.

And when he stands, I grip the edge of the sofa. I watch those broad, strong hands work the button of his pants open. Then the zipper. Finally, he pushes the pants, underwear, and all down to his ankles.

He stands in front of me, hands hanging by his sides, watching me. Watching my reaction. My face. My lips as they drop open. My eyes, as they follow the movement of his long, hard cock as it bobs as if to say hello. My breath catches, but I can't look away.

It's big. Massive, even.

And I ache. I'm so fucking empty, and I need it. Now. Right this second. It needs to be inside me, so I can feel the length and thickness of it buried between my legs.

Dragging my eyes up to his, I reach up to wrap my fingers around his cock. Warm, silken skin throbs beneath my touch, and before I know what I'm doing I find myself bringing my lips to it.

There's moisture beading at the tip, and I suddenly need to know what it tastes like. I need to have him on my tongue, just as he has me. I need to share everything with him.

I don't even know him, but does it matter? There's something happening between us. A union. Something *real*. It's not about titles or nobility. There's a connection between us that started the moment our eyes met across the ballroom.

He understands me, down to my core. He knew how I felt about the Count. He made me feel safe and comfortable when I needed it most. He brought me to this place, to play an instrument I've only dreamed of.

Why resist now? Why deny myself the pleasure I know he wants to give? It might be my only chance. After Maggie's married, I'm next.

When I lick the tip of his cock, feeling the tautness of his crown, we both let out a groan. I drop my lips open and take him in my mouth, finally tasting that salty, needy arousal.

The Duke sighs, cupping my cheek with his hand. He pushes himself deeper in my mouth, letting out a low sigh. "This isn't how I expected tonight to go," he says softly.

I moan in response, because it's the only thing I can do. The hum of my voice against his shaft makes him groan again, his hold on my head tightening ever so slightly. I let my fingers run up his strong thighs, feeling the sparse, dark hair beneath my palms. I grip his hips, bringing one hand around his shaft and the other crawling up his stomach.

Before I can stop him, the Duke wraps his fingers in my hair and pulls my head back. His length falls from my mouth with a soft pop.

I lift my eyes to meet his. "What's wrong?" It's almost a whine. I want more. I want to give him what he gave me. I want to taste his orgasm on my tongue and know that I made him do it.

I'm not usually like this. I've never gotten naked with someone I just met. I've never sucked a man's cock at a royal event or let him spread me wide and devour me.

But I'm not going to stop now—and neither is he.

Hooking his arms around my legs, the Duke yanks me forward on the sofa. I fall back, catching myself against the cushions as he kneels, letting his hands sweep up my thighs and over my stomach.

"What's wrong is that if you had your lips around my cock for another second, I was going to come all over that pretty tongue of yours."

The Duke's eyes are dark. I can't even see the green in them right now. All I see is desire. His tip teases my opening as his eyelids flutter, a sigh slipping through his lips.

"Tell me you're on the pill. Tell me you want this."

"I'm on the pill," I answer. I glance at him through my lashes. "I want this."

Desperately.

His face grows serious, his hands running back and forth over my thighs as he holds them up, my calves resting on his shoulders.

"I've been hard since the moment I laid eyes on you," he growls. "I thought I'd be fucking my fist to the memory of you for the rest of the year. I never thought I'd get the real thing."

"Number one, I'm not a thing," I say, wiggling my hips to try to feel more of him. "Number two, be quiet, Your Grace, and fuck me already."

Who is this person that's taken over my body? Who is this woman who's needy and dirty and wet? When did I become her?

The Duke's eyes darken as a wicked, wild look crosses his face.

With one movement of his hips, he drives himself inside me. I'm so wet he slides in easily, but he's still so big it hurts. It hurts...until it doesn't.

No, that's not pain anymore. Oh, no. Not pain. That's something else. My eyes widen. It's good. I like that. A lot.

He pushes deep inside me and I gasp, closing my eyes to enjoy this moment. The emptiness is gone. The ache has disappeared. I'm so deliciously filled—with *him*. The Duke rocks his hips back and forth as I moan, my lips dropping open. I reach for the edge of the sofa. I need to brace myself for this.

Heath clamps one arm across my legs, holding them against his torso as he drives into me. A grunt escapes him, and I love it. I love the noises. I love knowing he's losing control. With my legs pinned I know I'm tight around him, and I can see pleasure rippling across his features.

And me?

My body's on fire. My veins are full of molten lava, being pumped to every corner of my being. I can't breathe. I can't think. I can't even remember my own name.

When I close my eyes, I still see him. Heath. The Duke. *My* Duke.

The man who makes me see stars. The man who sets me alight and reminds me what it's like to be a woman. The man who thought of fucking his fist to the memory of me. Those strong, broad hands wrapped around his shaft, his eyes closed, chest heaving, thinking of *me*.

Why is that so hot?

I open my eyes to see him watching me, his eyes dark. With one hand still clamped over my legs he leans over me, thrusting deeper. I moan. His free hand finds my breast and he tweaks my nipple softly, then harder. I gasp, rocking my hips against him and not even caring that I'm grunting and moaning and huffing like never before.

"You like my cock inside you?" he asks, his voice low. Commanding.

I moan, nodding.

"Say it."

"I love it. I love your cock inside me." Dirty, dirty words. Heat rips through my core when they come out of my mouth, but they're true. I love his cock inside me. I love feeling every inch of it stretching me. Owning me. Marking me.

When the Duke reaches down between my legs and rolls his thumb over my clit, I come apart. A cry falls from my lips as the Duke tries to shush me, but I'm gone. I can't think. I have no control. I pant his name, coming on his cock as a smile stretches over his lips. He whispers a thousand dirty things to me, pumping me so full that one orgasm bleeds into the next.

Then, I feel it. The tightening in his shaft. The thick, throbbing spurts. The tension ratcheting in his body. I watch the slackness of his jaw and the drooping of his eyelids. And I *feel* it. I feel his orgasm lashing inside me, hot and strong and mine. It belongs to me. To tonight. To this moment that we're sharing.

As his hips rock one last time and his hands sweep over my body, I let out a long sigh. The Duke lets my legs drop open and, still joined to me, leans down to kiss me hard. I wrap my arms around his neck and my legs around his waist, tasting my first orgasm on his lips.

When the Duke pulls away, he lets out a slow exhale, staring deep in my eyes. "You're special, Ada Belcourt. I haven't felt like that in...ever."

A blush stains my cheeks. "I was that good, was I?" I grin, but I know right away it was the wrong thing to say.

His face falls, and a bit of stone returns to his features. The Duke wasn't talking about sex. He wasn't talking about an orgasm. This was something more for him.

And me?

What does this mean to me?

Is this really just a last chance at a dirty fuck? Is this me letting go before my inevitable betrothal to some old, rich man?

Or is there something that drew me to the Duke? This connection between us...could it be real?

I don't even know. I run my fingers over his temples, leaning my forehead against his. "I don't want to go back out there," I whisper. "I want to stay here with you forever."

He closes his eyes, nodding gently. "Me too."

"But..." I sigh.

"But we have to."

He pulls away from me, and I miss him already. He pulls his pants on, then walks over to the piano and picks my dress up off the floor. The silky fabric doesn't wrinkle, thankfully, and the Duke helps me slip it back over my body. He zips it up and spins me around, wrapping his arms around my waist. His lips drop to mine and I inhale another kiss, not wanting this to end.

"I want to see you again," he whispers against my lips.

I nod. "Me too."

I watch him pull his shirt on over his shoulders, sad that I no longer get to stare at his chest. He closes the buttons carefully, then moves to his bowtie, and finally I drag my eyes away from his body and hunt for my underwear. After a few fruitless minutes, I walk to a tall mirror on the other side of the room.

My hair is a mess. I take a tiny comb out of my purse and do my best to get my dark locks back into place, then move to fix my makeup. With only a small compact and a lipstick to work with, I look nowhere near as put together as I did when I walked in, but it'll have to do.

The Duke appears behind me, running his hands over my hips. His eyebrows jump up, meeting my gaze in the mirror. "No panties?"

I bite my lip. "I don't see them anywhere."

He grins, arching a brow. "Leave them. I like the thought of you naked under that dress. Some confused staff member will find them eventually and wonder what happened in here."

I blush, wanting to protest. I stop myself, though, and let him lead me from the room. My nakedness feels like another secret only he and I share.

When his hand is on the doorknob, I grab his arm.

"Wait." He frowns when I pull out my phone, flicking to the camera app. "Selfie," I explain.

"Do you do this with all your conquests?"

"Only you," I grin. I snap a picture, checking it quickly, then sending it to Kiera. I give the Duke a wink, then we exchange phone numbers.

My heart flutters as he types his number into my phone. He wants to see me again. He's giving me his number. This is happening.

A tiny voice at the back of my head asks, *What if I'm not destined for a loveless marriage?*

I try to push the thought down, but it screams louder. What if I could have it all? Someone like Heath who's handsome and accomplished *and* a good match. From what I've seen tonight, the stories about him can't be true. He's solitary, sure, and he doesn't leave his estate very often...

...but he's been hurt. His whole family passed away a few years ago, right around Christmastime. That's got to be traumatizing.

It doesn't mean he has women delivered to his home for debauched orgies...does it? He could be completely normal. This could be the start of something good.

As we walk back to the party, his back is straight and his face is shuttered. The picture of decorum.

Me, on the other hand? I'm pretty sure I look like I just got royally screwed.

9

ADA

My legs shake as I walk back to the ballroom, my heels echoing against the marble floors. I feel my nakedness with every step, a constant reminder of what I just did.

Oh, my God. What did I just do?

My cheeks burn. Resting my fingertips in the Duke's elbow, my heartbeat roars.

As we approach the tall double doors that open onto the ballroom, I can see guests standing on the other side. No one has spotted us yet, but judging by the attention we got on the dance floor, I know our entrance won't go unnoticed.

Heath must feel me stiffen, because he leans toward me. His scent envelops me, soothing my fraying nerves. "You are magnificent," he says in a low voice. "Don't let anyone make you feel otherwise."

I flick my gaze to his, expecting to see mirth dancing in his eyes. They're serious. He thinks I'm magnificent? No one's ever said anything like that to me before.

A smile slides over my lips as I duck my chin, straightening up as we walk through the arched doorway. As expected, a few heads turn. Eyebrows arch. Whispers are made behind raised palms. More heads turn to look. And on, and on, like a ripple through the crowd.

But I keep my spine straight and find Rhoda nearby. I slip my hand out of the Duke's elbow, turning to face him. "Thank you for showing me the piano room," I say loud enough for people to hear. "It was beautiful." I give him a curtsy and a polite smile.

The Duke's eyes flash. Broken, green glass stares back at me, his eyes drifting down my body. Embers burn in my veins, reminding me of what we were doing just moments ago. When I rise from my curtsy, the Duke catches my hand in his. He lays a soft, chaste kiss on my fingers, then releases them.

The distance between us feels like a chasm, but I turn away from him and head for Rhoda. I can feel the Duke's gaze on my back as I walk away. Other guests step out of my way, and I feel an odd sort of power coursing through me. Usually, unless I'm on stage performing, I hate being stared at. I hate crowds. I hate events.

Now?

I relish the surprised expressions on courtiers' faces. I love the way they look at me, and I love knowing I have a secret that no one but the Duke and I share.

When I reach Rhoda, she stares at me with wide eyes. "Where were you?"

"The Duke showed me the late Queen Mother's piano. He knew I was a concert pianist and thought I'd appreciate it. Apparently his family built it for the royal family as a wedding present."

Rhoda stares at me, her eyes boring into mine. "There's something you're not telling me."

I smooth my hands over my silver dress, nodding to a waiter who presents me with a tray of champagne flutes. I accept one between delicate fingers, taking a sip before shrugging. "I don't know what you want me to say."

"I want you to explain why the Duke of Blythe—the man who hasn't left his estate in *months*, and definitely hasn't danced at an official event since he was prepubescent, grabbed you in the middle of the dance floor, twirled you around, then whisked you away." She flicks her hair over her shoulder, arching a brow.

"Maybe he likes to dance. No one knows anything about him except what's in the tabloids and what old, bored ladies gossip about when they have high tea."

Rhoda snorts, shaking her head. "Dukes don't just start dancing at royal balls after years of standing against the walls." She glances across the room, trying to see Heath in the crowd. Then, ducking her head toward me, "What's he like?"

"The Duke?"

"No, your father." She rolls her eyes. "Yes, the Duke! I've heard so many things about him. They say he uses sex as a coping mechanism ever since..." Her voice trails off. Anyone in Farcliff could fill in the blanks. Ever since his beloved brother overdosed. Ever since his parents died. Ever since he inherited the estate and stopped attending society events. Ever since Blythe pianos stopped being built.

I take another sip of champagne, keenly aware of how little I've eaten tonight. It's going straight to my head. I glance across the room, my eyes immediately finding the Duke's. A rush of heat spreads through my core, and I remember I'm not wearing any underwear.

As his eyes drift down my dress, I know he's thinking the

same. Replaying the past hour of our lives in his head, just as I am. Remembering what it felt like to have his lips against mine. His hands on my body. His cock buried inside me.

I clear my throat, turning to Rhoda. "He's...interesting." I try to keep my voice neutral.

How can I explain that the Duke is completely addictive? I'm consumed by the thought of him already. I need to know everything there is to know about him. I need to know why he retreated away from society. Why he chose to come back today. Why he took interest in me.

I need to know if he truly thinks I'm magnificent, or that's just something he tells people. Was I just a coping mechanism during a very difficult evening?

Rhoda blows out a breath. "Interesting? You're going to have to give me more than that. What did he say? Was he polite? Rude? Abrasive?"

"He was well-mannered," I say, remembering the way he told me to beg for his cock. "Classy." Especially when he fisted his hands in my hair and tugged hard.

Rhoda arches an eyebrow.

I relent, knowing I need to give her more details. "I don't think the rumors have been kind to him. He's spent the past few years away from this type of event, and I don't think he particularly enjoys being here tonight." I pause, chewing the inside of my lip. "I'd like to see him again."

My friend's eyes flash as a blush spreads over my cheeks and neck, and all the way down my chest. I duck my head, shaking it gently until I hear her squeal. She grabs my arm, leaning close. "He's trouble, Ada. You know that, right?"

When I glance at her, Rhoda's eyes are shining. I bite my lip and grin. "Trouble isn't always bad, is it?"

We're both giggling when I hear my mother clear her

throat behind me. I turn to see her, my father, and Count Gregory standing there. I straighten up, letting my smile slip off my face.

I give them all a small curtsy, if only to buy time to compose myself. "Mother," I nod.

"Count Gregory has been kind enough to invite us to his Christmas dinner party in two weeks' time," she says, giving me a loaded look. "Isn't that wonderful?"

Dread creeps through my stomach as I swallow down the discomfort rising in my throat. More time with Count Gregory? More hours spent in his company? And I'm assuming Maggie will be there, too—I'll have to watch her interact with him, knowing he gives me the creeps.

But I paint a polite smile on my lips and turn to face the Count. "That's very kind of you," I say. "I'm sure it will be a wonderful evening."

"If you and your sister are in attendance, I have no doubt it will be." He catches my hand and lays a kiss on my fingers.

My body screams, yelling at me to pull away and maybe slap him across the face for good measure. I push the instinct down and wait for him to drop my hand, flicking my eyes to the corner where the Duke of Blythe was standing before.

He's watching us, a dark expression in his eyes.

Is it wrong that I like it? I like knowing he's jealous and angry and protective. I like knowing he's watching me, and that he doesn't like Count Gregory, either. In a room full of people who hide their true intentions and opinions as a matter of principle, it's refreshing to see someone who's honest.

My mother says something that I don't quite hear, and conversation starts up between us. My eyes flit to Rhoda, who arches a brow. She saw the look on the Duke of Blythe's face.

Leaning into my ear, she whispers, "You are going to have to tell me *everything*."

I shake my head, hiding a grin behind my hand. When I glance back across the room, the Duke is giving a low bow to Prince Damon, the King's younger brother. Prince Damon has his arm slung around Princess Dahlia, whose pastel pink hair is twisted into a complicated braid. The two look completely at ease with each other, and my heart tugs.

Just like the King and Queen, Prince Damon and Dahlia found love where they shouldn't have.

Will I ever have what they have? What the King and Queen have?

Gulping, I turn back to my parents, the Count, and Rhoda. The royal family can do what they want—including marry for love. The only one who hasn't found love yet is Prince Gabriel, all the way out at Westhill Castle, hiding away from royal life. He's a recluse like the Duke, with just as many dark rumors swirling around him and his past. Maybe the two of them would get along.

"We really should be going," my mother says, giving me a loaded look. Did she see me leave and come back with the Duke?

Who am I kidding? Of course she did. The entire guest list knows by now. They probably know how long I was away from the main ballroom down to the second. I'm sure there are rumors swirling already.

As I give Rhoda a hug goodbye, promising to talk to her during the week, I can't quite keep the smile from my face.

I don't care about rumors. I don't care about gossip. Tonight was incredible. I'll cherish the memory of it forever. A small, forbidden fantasy I didn't even know I had came true tonight.

And maybe I'll get to see the Duke again. Live out another

fantasy. Feel like a woman once more, before my inevitable betrothal to someone like Count Gregory.

Unless... I glance in the Duke's direction, hoping that maybe we can have something more—but he's gone. I shake my head, pushing the thought aside. I should just cherish tonight, not hope for things that won't happen.

10

ADA

KIERA SQUEALS when she hears us walk through the front door, flying down the hallway toward me. She throws her arms around my waist, squeezing tight. "You met him! What's he like?"

"Very handsome," I answer, feeling my mother's hawk-eyed stare on my back. The drive home was pointedly quiet, and I know she's waiting for the right moment to ask me exactly where I disappeared to with the Duke.

"I can't believe you met him. And he's smiling in the picture! I've never seen a picture of him smiling. Not since he was a kid, anyway." Kiera stares at her phone screen, shaking her head. "You're amazing."

I smile, looking over her shoulder to stare at the photo I sent her earlier. My gut clenches, remembering exactly where we were when that picture was taken.

Following Kiera back to the living room, I find Maggie asleep on the sofa. Her moon boot is still propped up on a cushion, and even in her sleep she looks elegant and put-together.

She blinks her eyes open when we enter, smiling softly. "I heard you made quite the splash." She grins, wiping her eyes.

"News travels fast," I say, taking a seat near her injured leg. My dress crinkles around my legs, and I remember I'm not wearing underwear. I should change.

I pull out my phone, staring at the dark screen. No text from the Duke. I try to ignore the disappointment squeezing my heart.

It's been, what, an hour? Why would he text me now? Why would he text me at all?

If Rhoda's right, he uses sex to get over his demons. Maybe that's all tonight was for him. A quick fuck to forget about the anniversary of the death of his entire family. Telling me he wanted to see me again was just good manners.

Right?

Or are my feelings true? There was *something* between us. Some sort of force that made our eyes meet across the room. An energy that flowed through us when we danced. And after, when we were alone...

Well, that was special. I've never experienced anything like it.

Shaking the thought away, I lean against the sofa and listen to my little sister tell me about her friends' reaction to the photo. My eyelids feel heavy, and a soft smile tugs at my lips. A big fire is blazing in the fireplace, making me feel warm and comfortable and happy.

My mother enters the room, already changed out of her gown and in a matching set of silk pajamas with a long robe tied loosely at the waist. Her updo has been unpinned and makeup removed, and she looks like my mother again. I'm reminded that the image of the noble Duchess of Belcourt is just that—an image. One we need to uphold by marrying the right men.

Mother looks at Kiera. "Bedtime."

Kiera sighs, closing her laptop and rolling her eyes. "Soon I'll be at college, and you won't be there to tell me my bedtime."

"Maybe it's not a good idea to send you there when you're only fifteen." My mother gives her a pointed stare, tilting her head.

Kiera drops her chin to her chest and stands up, waving at Maggie and me before heading out the door.

My mother turns to us, tightening her robe around her waist. "Count Gregory has invited you both to his Christmas dinner in two weeks."

Maggie sits up, wincing as she moves her broken ankle. I help her adjust the cushions, giving her an encouraging nod.

My mother levels us with a stare. "I expect you both to act like the ladies you are. No sneaking off with Dukes." Her eyes shift to me.

My cheeks burn hotter than they have in years. I stare at the carpet.

She looks at Maggie. "The Count seemed quite pleased with Ada, so we can assume the betrothal is still in the cards, despite your sister's little disappearing act. His Christmas party will be crucial in making sure this happens."

"I understand." Maggie folds her hands in her lap, looking every bit a lady, even with a broken ankle.

"This is important, girls," my mother says. "Kiera deserves the best, and we want to be able to send her to a good university. Count Gregory has contacts at all the top schools. He's made donations to our number one pick for the past thirty years, and the dean of Farcliff University might be at his dinner party, too. You understand how important this is?"

Maggie nods again, her eyes downcast. Her long, thick lashes fan over her cheeks, and my heart squeezes painfully.

She's sacrificing so much for Kiera. For all of us. By marrying Count Gregory, she's choosing our family's reputation over her own future. Kiera's education over the chance at a loving marriage.

Would I be able to do the same? Can I stand the thought of my sister giving up her whole future for us?

I put my hand over her good leg, squeezing gently.

She looks at me, nodding, then turns to Mother. "We won't let you down."

"Good." My mother gives us a curt nod, then walks over to the sofa and places a kiss on each of our heads. I feel like a little girl again, and not a celebrated concert pianist with a bachelor's degree.

Sadness clings to my spirit when I look at my sister, who looks resigned and calm and ready to face the weight of her obligations. She's braver than I am.

Glancing at my phone, all I see is a dark screen. If things between the Duke of Blythe and me were ever to work out, would Maggie have to go through with this marriage? Could I save her from a lifetime of duty?

I can't think like that. I had one night with the Duke. *Heath.* Even now, after a couple of hours, it feels wrong to call him by his first name—even in my head. We aren't that familiar with each other. We had a fun, memorable Christmas ball at the palace. That's all.

Right?

I GO to bed and dream of him.

11

HEATH

I LIE AWAKE all night thinking of Ada. I spend the entire next day staring at my phone, wondering if I should send her a message.

I want to. I'm dying to. My fingers itch to find her number and tell her I can't get her out of my head.

But I hold back. I heard Count Gregory invited Ada to his Christmas party, and I know what that means. He's making a move. One Belcourt daughter isn't enough—he wants to have his pick.

Typical Gregory. I'd wring the man's neck if I could do it without going to jail.

But murder won't do. I don't want to kill him. I want to ruin his reputation. Expose him for the garbage he is and show his precious society that he's scum. Clear my brother's name. Avenge my parents' death.

My stomach clenches. I hate that man. He took everything from me, and now he's taking Ada, too.

I never thought I'd meet a woman who makes the world seem brighter. I never thought I'd have a night like last night.

One that makes me feel full and sated, instead of empty and sad.

She's a drug. I'm hooked.

But I can't text her—not while her life is intertwined with the Count's. Not before I bring down my accusations on him.

I just need a bit more time.

Instead of calling Ada, I call my lawyer and let him talk some sense into me. I review all the communications I've had with the King and prepare to meet with him and tell him what I've found out about Count Gregory.

I do my best to distract myself with anything and everything that isn't Ada.

It doesn't help.

As it turns out, I do fuck my fist to the thought of her. Again, and again, and again.

12

ADA

THE DAYS DRAG ON. Hour by hour. Minute by minute. I check my phone a thousand times an hour, my heart trilling every time I have a new notification. On Wednesday, I meet Rhoda for coffee, and she catches me glancing at the blank screen.

"Loverboy Blythe?" she asks, arching an eyebrow.

I blush. I'm doing a lot of that lately.

Rhoda leans back in her chair, her long, fine manicured nails drumming on the surface of the table. The big rock on her finger glitters at me, winking in the light of the café, reminding me of the world we really live in.

One where marriages are matches, and love is nothing but a fantasy.

"You like him," she announces, almost accusing me.

I shake my head. "I don't even know him."

"What exactly happened in that piano room?"

"I played Chopin."

"And then he played Chopin all over your body?"

I swear my cheeks are just permanently red now. I shake my head. "That doesn't even make sense, Rhoda."

"Something happened. You can't hide it from me." She grins.

"We talked." I don't know why I don't want to tell her every sordid detail. We used to share all kinds of stories. When we were in college, we'd come back from a night out and tell each other a play-by-play of everything that happened.

But this feels different. What happened between the Duke and me feels too special to share. It would ruin it somehow.

"You exchanged numbers?" Rhoda sips her coffee, staring at me with her sharp blue eyes.

I nod.

"He hasn't contacted you?"

"It's been four days," I say, sounding whinier than I mean to.

"So text him." She shrugs, nodding to my phone.

I close my eyes, shaking my head. "I can't."

"Why not?"

"What if I misread the situation? What if he just gave me his number to be polite?"

I want to see you again. I can still hear his voice in my head. *You are magnificent.* That didn't sound like mere politeness.

"What's the worst that can happen? He stays on his estate ninety-nine percent of the time, anyway. It's not like you'll run into him at a restaurant or anything. Just send him a message."

Biting my lip, I pick up my phone. I glance at my friend, who has laughter dancing in her eyes. "What do I say?"

She tilts her head, running her fingers along the base of her coffee cup. She motions for my phone, and I clutch it to my chest.

"Don't you dare send anything without letting me see it first."

"I would never." She grins.

Reluctantly, I hand her my phone. Her fingers fly over the screen for a moment, and then she hands it back to me. "There."

Ada: Hey!

I lift my eyes to Rhoda's, frowning. "'Hey?' That's it?"

"Keep it simple," she answers, shrugging. "Men are uncomplicated creatures."

I chew my lip, staring at the screen. I can't send 'Hey!'— I'm not some guy on Tinder with the intellect of a sea slug. I erase it, type another message, and hit send before I can change my mind.

Ada: Have you recovered from the trauma of a public appearance?

I turn my phone around and show Rhoda, who nods appreciatively. "Cheeky, funny, and a little flirty. You're a natural."

"I don't know how to flirt."

"Oh, please." She laughs.

My phone buzzes, and Heath's name flashes on the screen. My eyes widen. "It's him."

"Already?" Rhoda makes a *grabby-hands* gesture at me, nodding at my phone. "Read it or let me see. Don't just sit there! I haven't had this much fun since college." She laughs, glancing at the ring on her finger. Sadness flashes across her face and disappears again, almost too fast for me to notice.

Just like Maggie, she's chained to her duty.

I swipe my phone open and read the message.

Heath: Barely. Thinking of you sitting at the piano has helped.

My hands tremble when I show Rhoda, who squeals

79

when she reads it. She purses her lips, shaking her head. "Ada Charlotte Belcourt, you'd better tell me exactly what happened in that piano room right now, or else I'm not sure we can be friends any longer."

I laugh, reading the Duke's message again. I lift a shoulder in a shrug. "We may have kissed."

It's not *not* true.

Rhoda's eyes are massive. Her lips drop open as her hands splay on the table, waiting for me to continue.

I close my eyes, shaking my head. "I don't know. He said he wanted to see me again. I don't really know what that means."

"I think it means he wants to see you again," Rhoda answers slowly, enunciating every word. She laughs, shaking her head. "Trust you to ensnare a reclusive Duke. You'll end up better off than any of us without even trying. Just like college."

I frown. "What do you mean, just like college?"

"Um, have you forgotten the gaggle of men that followed you everywhere? How they hung on every word? How they came to your performances? I'm pretty sure you single-handedly caused a resurgence in the popularity of classical music."

I wave a hand, shaking my head. "I had friends."

"Mm," Rhoda answers, shaking her head. She nods to my phone. "Don't leave the man hanging. I guarantee you he's staring at his phone right now, waiting for you to answer."

I take a deep breath and type out the first thing that comes to mind.

Ada: I could play for you again, if you think it would help your mental health.

I hope he can hear the grin in my text. I press send, putting my phone face down on the table. I look at Rhoda. I need to change the subject, if only to regain control over my racing heart. "How about you? Tell me about your engagement. When's the wedding?"

"Next June." She gives me a tight smile. "My family is happy with the marriage. The Duke of Harbor is a nice man. He has a property near Westhill Castle which he says is beautiful in the summertime. That's where the wedding will be."

I smile. "I'm glad for you, Rhoda. You deserve to be happy."

My friend reaches over to me, placing her hand on mine. "I'm doing this because it's expected of me, and it's the best option for my family. But you"—she pauses, glancing at my phone—"you could have something more."

"It's just a couple of text messages," I say, shaking my head, even though her words feed a deep well of excitement in my gut.

What if it were more? What if things with the Duke were real?

My phone buzzes, and Rhoda gives me a meaningful glance. *It's more than a couple of text messages*, the look says.

Heath: Tonight. I can show you the last piano my parents built.

I close my eyes for a moment, trying to contain the emotion bubbling up inside me. Maybe Rhoda's right. Maybe there's something between the Duke and me that could be more.

I could have it all—and save Maggie from a loveless marriage while I'm at it.

13

ADA

A FEW HOURS LATER, Richard, our house manager, knocks on the sitting room door. When he introduces the Duke of Blythe, all heads lift in surprise.

My heart takes off, carrying my breath away with it. Kiera lets out a squeal, clapping her hand over her mouth. Maggie stares at me, asking a thousand questions with her eyes.

But it's my mother who shoots me the heaviest glare. It's gone in an instant, when she stands up to greet the Duke.

"Your Grace," she says, expertly hiding the surprise in her voice. "How lovely of you to visit."

As if this isn't completely out of the ordinary. As if he visits all the time.

The Duke bows to my mother and father, then moves to shake my father's hand. His eyes find mine, a grin tugging at the corner of his lips. My head is spinning so hard I don't even hear the pleasantries exchanged.

The Duke is here. In my living room. Talking to my family.

When he told me he wanted to meet me tonight, I thought—actually, I don't know what I thought. I didn't think he'd walk in and start talking to my father about the weather. Maybe I expected him to stop the car outside and honk the horn, or something.

But he wouldn't do that. He's a Duke. My family is noble. There are conventions to adhere to.

My mother straightens up. "Your Grace..." She glances at me, frowning ever so slightly. "To what do we owe the honor?"

"Ah," the Duke replies, his soft lips curving. I want to kiss them again. I want to taste his tongue against mine and curl my fingers into his shirt. He glances at me. "I thought Lady Belcourt would have told you. I offered to show her the last piano my parents built before they"—he clears his throat—"before they passed. She had expressed interest in seeing it at the Christmas ball last weekend."

"Oh." My mother's eyebrows jump.

A flush rips up my neck and bursts into flame over my cheeks. I hate that I'm blushing right now. I'm a young woman in my mid-twenties. I shouldn't be blushing because a man wants to spend time with me.

But he's not just a man, and I'm not just a young woman. There are conventions in our society, and this visit is... unusual. Or at least, it's unexpected.

My father nods. "Well, we won't keep you. Do you need us to send a car, Ada?"

I shake my head. "That won't be necessary, Father."

The Duke extends his arm, and I slide my hand into the crook of his elbows. As soon as I touch him, a rush of heat spins through my insides. He's close enough to smell. To feel the heat of his body. To remember what it felt like to be naked together.

When we get to the front door, Heath helps me put a jacket on, smiling as I stuff a woolen hat over my ears.

Richard, now wearing white gloves and a crisp jacket he hadn't been wearing before, bows to us and opens the front door. The Duke's hand materializes on my lower back as he leads me to the car, and another thrill rushes down through my thighs.

I like the way he touches me. Gentlemanly. Chastely. Appropriately—but as a constant reminder of what those hands felt like when they sank into my thighs and pulled me close. A sleek silver vehicle gleams in our driveway. Every part of it is shiny and clean, and I wonder how he managed to keep it that way while driving through the snowy, slushy streets.

Heath opens the car door for me, his eyes flicking down to my lips. At some point he slipped leather gloves over his hands, and I watch the way the fabric stretches when he curls his fingers over the top of the door. Every detail makes my body wind tighter. Every hint of his delicious male scent. Every blink of his thick, dark lashes. Every gaze that drifts over my face, my body—it all sends me into a tailspin.

When the Duke closes my door and walks around the front of the vehicle, his steps are steady and measured. He holds his chest high as his arms hang loosely by his sides. He walks as if he owns the world. Like he knows people would show him deference and give him whatever he wanted.

How could they not? The man exudes power.

When Heath slips into the car, he flashes a smile at me and I go soft around the middle. Every smile feels like a secret that he only shares with me. Letting my lips curl gently, I fiddle with the edge of my hat.

"Ready?"

"I can't believe I'll be going to the Blythe Estate," I say, letting my smile stretch wider. "I feel like I've been blessed by some higher power."

"No higher power." Heath chuckles. "Just me." Putting the car in gear, he starts to drive. The seat warms beneath me, and soon I'm unbuttoning my jacket and pulling my hat off my head. In the closeness of the vehicle, I feel the Duke's presence everywhere. It's like his energy expands to fill any space he's in. He's magnetic.

I can sense every movement of his body over the pedals, the gear shift, the steering wheel. When did driving a car become sexy? He's relaxed and in control, and it reminds me of the way he made love to me. Like it comes naturally to him.

When we turn off down a country road and come up to a set of tall gates, I shift in my seat, peering through the windshield.

"Looking for truckloads of women being delivered?" Heath doesn't hide the grin in his voice.

I throw him a glance. "Please."

He rewards me another panty-melting smile. Is it the heated seat that's making me so hot? Or is it just him?

Dusk is falling all around us, throwing warm colors across the sky. In front of us, a huge mansion is silhouetted against the sunset. My heart thumps.

As far as I know, no guest has been here in months. Years, maybe. The Duke hasn't attended any official events apart from the Christmas ball, and hasn't received anyone from society here since his parents passed away. The estate has basically been cut off from all outside eyes. Curiosity burns in my stomach.

I'm worse than Kiera.

We park in a large garage, where an attendant appears at my door. Dressed in a crisp uniform, he opens the door for me and bows, helping me out of the car.

Heath tosses him the keys, glances at me, and jerks his head toward the door. "This way."

Once inside the house, another member of staff appears, helping me out of my jacket. Everything happens quickly. Efficiently. The staff seems well-trained and well-practiced. It's not until the man taking my jacket gives me a curious glance that I realize this situation is unusual.

"Come," Heath says, extending his hand.

When my palm slips over his, a delicious current of heat skips across my skin. I fall into step beside him, feeling like this is the most natural place to be. Like I belong here, at his side.

Blythe Estate has been shrouded in mystery for the past four years, and I guess I expected it to be dark and dingy and mysterious.

It's not.

The hallways are wide and bright. Rooms we pass are well-kept and clean, as if the entire mansion is lived-in and loved. We pass pictures of the late Duke and Duchess of Blythe as well as Heath and his brother as children. The whole place feels warm and welcoming, with staff greeting us at every corner. Heath knows all their names.

There are touchscreens at the entrance to every room, and when we pass through a large foyer, I notice the lights brightening and dimming beside us. The whole place must have been rewired as a smart home, with sensors and pre-programmed settings made exactly to the Duke's preference.

He's not some brooding, mysterious Duke who retreated from civilization. He's just been living life on his terms.

Noticing my stares, Heath grins at me. "Not what you expected?"

"I thought this place would be haunted."

He gives me a sad smile, squeezing my palm. "I used to think it was."

Beneath the surface, Heath is a complicated patchwork of pain and love. I see glimpses of it when he drops his serious expression. Right now, his eyes linger on a large portrait of his family.

Giving his head a slight shake, he jerks his chin to a door at the end of the hall. "You'll love this piano," he says, pushing the tall, wide door open.

I gasp.

A huge room opens up before us, the walls and floor paneled in rich oak that makes my footsteps resonate. The acoustics in this space are insane. It looks like it was purpose-built for the huge grand piano that sits illuminated in the center of the room.

I drop Heath's hand, taking a few quick steps forward before pausing, afraid to touch the instrument. I turn to look at him, completely in awe.

I catch another glimpse of the man beneath the brooding exterior. His green eyes shine in the light of the room, watching me. His face is open. Hopeful.

I could fall in love with him when he looks at me like this. I might already have.

"My mother commissioned it from one of the master piano craftsmen they employed," Heath explains, taking long, measured steps toward me. He puts his hand on my back, leading me toward the instrument. "She used to sit in here and play for hours. I have it tuned every year, even though no one ever plays it."

"Heath..." My voice trails off, eyes glued to the piano. It's incredible. The cover has been opened and I peer inside, looking at the hundreds of strings stretched tight across the wide body. It gleams black and sleek, waiting to be played. I can tell without touching it that it's been made with love. Walking to the keys, I let my fingers drift over them, testing a chord out.

Rich, warm sound rings out. Chills rush down my spine. The keys have a wonderful weight to them, and the sound they produce makes my whole body thrum. I've never played anything like it.

Giving Heath a questioning glance, I see his eyes shining. He nods to the bench. We don't need to speak. I know he wants me to play.

This time he stands by the piano, watching my face. I don't feel nervous or embarrassed. I know playing this instrument is an honor that I don't deserve, but I'll do my best to try.

So, I play.

Music has a special ability to reach into my soul and dig out the purest of emotions. Playing an instrument like this one—in the Blythe Estate, under the watchful eyes of the Duke himself—heightens every sensation. I'm wound as tight as the strings of the piano, tugged by every note. My whole body becomes an extension of the music, and before I know it tears spill over my cheeks.

When the piece of music finishes, I stop playing and wipe my face. Gulping, I lift my eyes to the Duke's.

He stares at me like I just cracked his heart open. Lips parted, hand on his chest, eyes shining. I watch his chest heave as the air thickens between us.

His throat bobs as he swallows, and he runs a hand through his thick black hair. "My mother used to play that piece all the time," he says, emotion choking his words. "How did you..."

"I didn't," I whisper. "I'm sorry if I—"

"No," he answers. "It was perfect."

It only takes him two steps to reach me, and one swift movement to lift me off the bench. Pulling me into his chest, the Duke crushes his lips to mine. He kisses me hungrily, as if he needs me to live. Wrapped in his arms, he holds me close.

When we come up for air, I search his face. "Why did you wait for me to text you?"

It feels so good to be here, but I don't understand him. I don't understand what he wants from me. When we're together, it feels real—but the minute we're apart, it's like it never happened.

Heath's face tenses. He inhales, shaking his head, then rests his forehead against mine. "I wanted to leave the ball in your court. I didn't know if you'd want to see me again."

"You were scared." I grin, nudging him.

Heath huffs out a laugh, shrugging. "Can you blame me? Look at you." His hands sweep down my back, cupping my ass and pulling me into him.

I'm not sure it's true. There's something in his face that tells me he's holding back. Not telling me the whole truth. Is it just because I'm part of society and he isn't? He doesn't want to enter my world now that he's left it behind?

"I'd sit and listen to you play forever," he says, his lips brushing against mine.

I smile. "I have a concert in two and a half weeks."

"I'll be there."

I tilt my head to find his lips again. My fingers cling onto his shirt. I melt into him as my body heats up, every bit of me remembering what it felt like to be tangled in his arms. To feel his skin against mine. His tongue between my legs.

But before anything can happen, there's a knock on the doorframe. Someone clears their throat, clearly uncomfortable. The Duke and I separate, turning to the noise.

One of the members of staff is standing at the door, eyes

averted. "Your Grace," he says quietly, raising his eyes. Unspoken conversation happens, and Heath strides toward him. He leans his head near the other man's, listening to a few whispers.

I hear fragments. *His Majesty the King. Evidence. Investigation.*

What's that about?

Heath nods, then turns to me. His face is shuttered, once again wearing a mask of stone. "I'm sorry, Lady Belcourt. I have to attend to some urgent matters." He extends his hand toward me, and when I reach him he presses his lips to my fingers. "Mr. Seville will drive you home. I apologize."

With that, he gives me a quick bow and hurries down the hallway.

I stare after him, frowning, until the man clears his throat again and gestures for us to leave.

I don't see any sign of the Duke as I'm led back through the house and into the garages, and finally driven home.

Alone, empty, and vaguely embarrassed.

14

ADA

I DON'T HEAR from Heath after I leave his estate. Not. One. Word. A day passes, then two, then three. Pretty soon it's been ten days since I saw him, and I still haven't heard anything.

If he's waiting for me to text him again, he'll wait a long time. I'm not going to be the one to keep chasing him when he ignores me. If the *ball is in my court,* as he said, well I'm choosing not to play it. I have to have *some* kind of pride. I can't just go to his house, get kicked out, then come back begging for more.

I fill my days practicing for my last concert of the year, then spend time with my sisters.

On Saturday morning before Count Gregory's Christmas dinner party, I laze in Maggie's bedroom as she sorts through her walk-in closet. As I lie back on the sofa near the window, I try to wade through the mess in my mind. Between the Duke and our—ahem—*encounter* at the ball, the invitation to his place, and his sudden disappearance from my life, and not to mention the mess with Maggie's engagement to an old creep, I'm not feeling the holiday spirit.

"I wish I didn't have to wear this stupid moon boot," she

sighs, her voice muffled by the clothes in her closet. "It doesn't exactly go with any of these dresses."

"You'll look perfect," I reply. I watch as my sister comes back out holding two options. I nod to the black dress in her left hand. "Try that one."

When she disappears in the closet again to slip it on, I gather my courage. I need to talk to her about this betrothal, because I'm not sure it's the right decision. Sure, she needs to marry well. Count Gregory knows the deans at all the nearby colleges—and has contacts all throughout North America—but there must be some other way. Scholarships, maybe? Loans?

When Maggie reappears, looking gorgeous and respectable and every bit a royal, I smile. "Beautiful."

Her face falls. "You don't like it."

"It's not that."

"You've been grumpy ever since you came back from your date with the Duke. Aren't you ever going to tell me what happened? It was a week and a half ago."

"Nothing happened," I lie. "He showed me his piano."

"Is that a euphemism?"

I toss a cushion at her head. "You're supposed to be the respectable one, Maggie." I grin. "And *no*. Not a euphemism. It was the piano his mother had commissioned before..." I grimace. "Before she died."

"Oh," Maggie says. "And he hasn't called you since?"

"Nope." I pop the *p* as I say it. "Not even a message to apologize for basically kicking me out. Maybe I read the situation wrong," I answer. "Maybe he really did just want to show off his piano." I cut a glare in her direction. "Still not a euphemism."

Maggie laughs, adjusting the dress as she stares in a

mirror. She checks the back of it, trying to shift it so her moon boot doesn't stick out from underneath the hem.

I take a deep breath. "That's not what's on my mind, though."

"Oh?"

"It's about Count Gregory."

Maggie meets my gaze in the mirror, stilling her hands. "What about him?"

"I'm not sure you should go through with this."

"I'm not sure I have a choice."

"Of course you have a choice," I answer. "No matter what Mother says. You always have a choice. He just..." I suck a breath in through my teeth. "He gave me the creeps at the ball."

"He's harmless."

"Are you sure about that?" I chew my lip. "He was staring at me—it made the hairs on the back of my neck stand up."

Maggie drops her gaze, letting out a long breath. "Ada, I know you're worried. Maybe you don't understand the world we live in, but—"

"I understand perfectly. But I also understand that it's the twenty-first century, and no matter how badly we want Kiera to reach her full potential, there are other ways of going about it. You're signing your life away."

"You think I don't know that?" Maggie snaps. She takes a sharp breath, releasing it slowly. "I'm sorry. I didn't mean to be rude."

My heart breaks. My gentle, responsible sister is as worried about this as I am, but she's resigned herself to her fate. When her eyes lift up to meet mine, I see the truth in her face. She knows exactly what Count Gregory is like. She knows that she's signing up to, at best, tolerate a harem of mistresses. At worst, he'll demand her full attention. Mind and body.

Gross.

My sister is walking into this loveless marriage with her eyes wide open.

"Maybe we can figure something else out," I say softly.

"Like what? The Duke of Blythe? Last I checked he hasn't called you back."

Ouch. I wince.

Maggie turns toward me, dropping her shoulders. She comes to sit on the couch next to me, leaning her head on the back of the sofa. "I'm sorry," she says in a low voice. "That was mean of me."

"It's true," I admit. "I have no idea what's going on with the Duke. For all I know, I'll never see or speak to him again. Maybe one Christmas ball per decade is enough of an outing for him."

Maggie snorts. She turns to face me, reaching out to put her hand on top of mine. "Don't worry about me, Ada. I've thought about nothing else except my options for the past six weeks. I know what I'm getting into, and... I don't know. Maybe a part of me thinks the stability will be good. I won't have to worry about our parents losing our home or Kiera not being able to study. Maybe the Count and I can learn to love each other."

I give her a tight smile, but discomfort churns in my gut. I'm not sure the Count is capable of love. I only met him at the Christmas ball, but every instinct in me tells me she should run.

I shift on the sofa and groan, touching my chest. "My boobs are sore as hell."

"Period?"

"No," I say. "Not yet. I just feel...blah."

Maggie grimaces. "The Duke messed you up, Ada," Maggie says softly. "You haven't been the same since you met him."

I can't quite bring myself to meet my sister's eyes. She's right. Ever since I met the Duke, my life has been a series of highs and lows. Highs when I see him, and lows when he ignores me afterward. This past week has been particularly difficult. After being marched off his property and not hearing a word, my pride is more than a little wounded.

Am I really that naive? I really thought I was special?

Maggie squeezes my arm. "You'll feel better soon. Choose a comfy dress for tonight. You want to look through my stuff?"

"You're four inches shorter and twenty pounds lighter, and you're a ballerina." I grin. "Looking through your closet will probably make me feel worse. But thanks for the offer."

My sister reaches for me, wrapping me in a hug. "Thank you for worrying about me," she says, her voice muffled in my shoulder. "But believe me, I know what I'm doing."

She squeezes me tight, crushing my chest a little too hard. "Ow," I complain, pulling away.

My sister laughs, standing up again and letting out a long sigh. "I'll go with this black dress. At least it mostly conceals the moon boot."

With a tight smile, I nod. "Good choice."

WHEN WE ARRIVE at Count Gregory's mansion, Maggie gives my hand a squeeze. I nod to her, not quite able to wipe away my frown. We're greeted by staff and led inside, where our names are announced before being led to a huge living room. A dozen or so guests turn to look, and Count Gregory detaches himself from a conversation to greet us.

He says hello to my mother and father, then bows to my

sister and kisses her fingers. I brace myself for my own greeting. The Count's gaze slithers up my body and comes to rest on my eyes. His lips twitch as he dips his chin.

"Lovely to see you again, Lady Belcourt." He bows, dropping his lips to my fingers.

I give him the slightest curtsy, swallowing hostility. Maggie elbows me, and I manage to widen my smile. "We're very pleased to be here," I answer. "Merry Christmas."

The door behind us opens, and a footman announces another name. "The Duke of Blythe," he says, bowing and stepping aside.

My heart thunders as my stomach clenches. The Duke...is *here*?

When Heath steps into the doorway, I feel like I'm going to faint. Wearing a well-tailored suit and an irresistible scowl, the Duke's eyes find mine. Then, his gaze flits to the Count's hand, which somehow is resting on my mid-back. He must have seen me waver when the Duke walked in.

I take half a step away from the Count, trying to catch my breath. "Your Grace," I say, curtsying to the Duke.

He barely acknowledges me with a slight bow of his head, turning instead to the Count.

That stings. Not even a word of hello. My pride is taking a beating. I definitely read the situation wrong. The Duke wants nothing to do with me.

"Thank you for the invitation," Heath says to Count Gregory.

"I'm surprised to see you accepted," the Count replies through gritted teeth. The tension between the two men thickens, and my eyes jump from one to the other. Do they have a history?

"Wouldn't miss it for the world. I do love Christmas," the Duke replies, flicking his eyes back to me. His gaze sends heat sweeping over my body, and suddenly the room feels too warm. My dress is too tight. I need water, or food, or fresh air.

Maggie grabs my arm and yanks me away from the men, tilting her head to mine. "You have to tell me what's going on."

"I would if I knew," I hiss back, feeling the Duke's gaze on my skin. I force myself not to look back at him.

I'm not that desperate.

First he ignores me after the Christmas ball until I send him a message. Then he basically kicks me out of his house right after I get there. Now he barely says a word of hello?

How am I supposed to decipher that tangled web of messages? Does he like me or not? Is this some kind of game to him?

I gulp, accepting a glass of water from a passing waiter, ignoring the flutes of champagne on the tray. I have no desire to get well-acquainted with the Count's porcelain.

Two old duchesses walk up to my sister and me, crooning over us and asking Maggie about her broken ankle. I make sure the ladies are between me and the Duke, if only to shield myself from his gaze.

Or his glare, I should say. He's staring at me like he wants to murder me. What did I do wrong?

My cheeks burn. Even the tips of my ears feel hot. I ignore his stare, choosing instead to listen to the gossip from the two old ladies in front of me.

I can't get away from the Duke, though, because that's all they seem to want to talk about. "He hasn't attended any social gathering in four years, and now it's two within a month," one woman says, glancing over his shoulder. "And to come *here* of all places!"

I frown. "Why would coming here be particularly surprising?"

Lady Gertrude, the older of the two, snorts as she puts her hand to her pearl necklace. "There's no love lost between Count Gregory and the Duke."

"Why not?"

Maggie puts a sharp elbow between my ribs and throws me a loaded look, but I can't help it. I stare at the two ladies, waiting for an explanation.

"Well, with all the business with his brother and that experimental drug treatment..." Lady Gertrude trails off, turning to greet another guest. She makes a big show of turning her back to my sister and me, and I know I'm not going to get any more answers from her.

Looking at my sister, I frown. "What happened between the Duke's brother and Count Gregory? What's she talking about?"

Maggie shrugs. "I never heard anything. Probably just idle gossip."

I glance across the room to see storm clouds brewing over Count Gregory's head. He looks absolutely murderous. A chill skitters down my spine, and I shake my head. "Doesn't look like idle gossip."

Someone clears their throat behind me, and I turn to see the Duke standing there. My stomach clenches. That scent of his, so intoxicating, wraps around me like a warm fog. His eyes are dark and unreadable. When my gaze drifts over his broad shoulders, I remember what it felt like to be sheltered within his arms.

"Ada," he says softly. My sister stiffens at his familiar tone. "I'm sorry for the other evening. Mr. Seville told me you made it home safely."

"I did." My tone is frosty, but my body burns.

"Please understand that I had urgent business at the castle. I'm sorry for my rudeness."

At the castle?

I want to be mad at him. I hate these games we seem to be playing. I hate not knowing where we stand and what he wants. I'd like to turn my back on him and tell him to leave me alone, but my whole body is begging me to take a step closer and crush my lips to his.

My body and mind and heart are at war. I've known the man for two weeks, and I'm already knotted up in complicated feelings for him.

He lets out a long breath. "When I heard you were coming to the Count's holiday dinner, I knew I had to attend," he says, his voice a low growl.

My eyes flick to his. I don't understand the look on his face. Pain. Frustration. Anger. Did I make him angry? What could I have done wrong? He kicked me out of his house and didn't speak to me for ten days.

"You didn't have to do anything," I reply. "I know you had your own affairs to attend to. I don't need an explanation from you."

The skin around his eyes tightens as his lips drop open. He sucks in a breath, then gives me a curt nod. "I understand."

A bell rings, and it's time for dinner.

15

ADA

THE DUKE IS SEATED at the far end of the long dining table. The Count, unfortunately, sits down just opposite my sister and me. I catch the old man's gaze flicking to me one too many times, and I shift uncomfortably. Why is he staring so much? It's creepy.

Maggie looks like the perfect little lady she is. Poised and polite. Perfectly mannered and totally at ease. Is everything in her body not screaming at her to get out of here? How can she resign herself to this life?

Laughter booms at the opposite end of the long table, with Lady Gertrude hanging off the Duke of Blythe's arm. He flashes her a smile, and I watch the old lady melt. Jealousy rips through my core just as the Duke catches me staring.

I flush, dropping my eyes to my plate.

I'm jealous of an old woman? What's wrong with me?

"You two make a lovely sight," the Count says, looking at my sister and me. That same dirty feeling ekes into my veins, making me feel unwashed and uncomfortable.

Maggie answers something appropriate and polite, and I just push my chair back. "Excuse me."

Half-hearing the protests of my mother, I rush out of the dining room and try to find a bathroom. I open and close three doors before finding one that leads to a large, lush washroom, closing the door and leaning against the vanity.

Why is the Duke here? Why do my eyes always seem to be drawn to him? Why do I care if he's entertaining half the table, and not me?

I should never have slept with him. It's made a mess of my head, and I don't know how to make it right again.

The bathroom door opens. I yelp and open my eyes wide when the Duke steps inside, closing the door behind him.

"Ada," he says, and I melt at the sound of my name on his lips. His arm sweeps around my waist, catching me as I waver on my feet.

"What are you doing here?" I stammer.

"I was worried about you."

I scoff. "Why haven't you spoken to me, then? It's been nearly two weeks."

Heath's brows draw together, and his lips drop open. "There are things going on that I can't talk about. It's complicated."

"And that prevents you from speaking to me?"

He chews his lip, ducking his chin. "Yes."

I scoff, trying to push away from him. His arm loosens around my waist, but I don't quite have the courage to take a step back. I like his closeness a bit too much.

Lifting my eyes to his, I try to look for some sort of clue. "What's going on between us?"

The Duke's lips drop open and snap shut again. His hand slides from my lower back up my spine.

I step closer to him, pressing my chest against his. My breasts really are very sore. I ignore the pain, tilting my head as Heath sweeps his hand over my cheek.

"You look gorgeous tonight," he rasps.

I close my eyes, shaking my head. "Why are you saying that to me? Why talk to me at all? Aren't you just going to leave here and ignore me again?"

"The last thing I want to do is ignore you," he says, leaning his forehead against mine.

My knees knock. He's so close, and his body feels so good pressed up against mine. But we're in a bathroom in Count Gregory's mansion, and the Duke has been pretty much ignoring me for two weeks. Shouldn't I have a little pride? If he wants to be with me, don't I deserve more than stolen kisses at parties?

But then the Duke shifts his head and brushes his lips against mine. He parts them, sweeping his tongue across the seam of my mouth. I moan softly, already drunk on his kiss.

It feels too good in his arms. He feels too safe and warm and alive, and I'm too weak to resist.

Even when the Duke deepens the kiss, pressing me up against the vanity, I don't pull away. I know I should stop. I should have some pride. I should demand he take me out on a date or—at the very least—talk to me outside of a public event.

But his body is all hard planes and male strength. His lips are warm and wanting. Even when he grabs the fabric of my gown and rolls it up to my thighs, I can't quite bring myself to stop him. His fingers slide up my thighs as his kiss becomes more insistent.

"I came here to see you," the Duke whispers against my lips. "I don't want to be here, in this house, but I haven't been able to stop thinking about you."

"So why not call me?" I stare into his eyes. What does he mean, he doesn't want to be in this house? What happened between him and Count Gregory?

I try to look mad. I *should* be mad. I should be angry that he slept with me and hasn't spoken to me outside one quick visit to his house. I should be furious. I should have some scrap of pride and take myself away from here. My body betrays me, though. My feet step wider to allow his hand to slip between my thighs. When he feels the heat of my core, he groans.

"I wasn't lying when I said you were magnificent, Ada," he growls, nipping at my bottom lip. "I want to see you every day. I want to wake up next to you and fuck you senseless every single morning." His hand tugs at my panties, pulling the damp fabric to the side. When he feels my wetness, he groans again. His fingers slide through my arousal, and I can't lie. I can't pretend to be cold with him when my body is an inferno. I can't pretend to push him away when all I want is more.

His fingers slip inside me as he whispers in my ear. His words make my anger evaporate. *Dirty girl. You're so hot for me. Come on my fingers. You're mine.*

I shouldn't want this, but I can't deny it. I should push him away and tell him I deserve more, but I just crumple in his hands and give him the orgasm he asks for. I come on his fingers, clinging onto his shoulders and panting his name.

When it's done, the Duke's eyes are shining. He lets my dress fall back down and lays a soft kiss on my lips, groaning. The bulge in his pants presses against my thigh, but he makes no move to unbuckle his trousers.

"I can't stop thinking about you, Ada."

"Could have fooled me," I quip, but my voice is weak. Every time I've seen him, he's made me feel like the most special woman in the world.

But when I say goodbye to him when this dinner is over, will he even try to talk to me again?

Heath lays a soft kiss on my lips, then jerks his head to the door. "They'll be wondering where you are."

"But not you?"

"I need a minute." He nods to his crotch, and heat blooms across my cheeks. His hand drifts over my cheek. "I'll see you at your concert, if not sooner."

"You're coming to watch me play?" My voice sounds small.

He nods. "Wouldn't miss it for the world." He kisses me, then pulls back and jerks his chin to the door. "Go."

I bite my lip, nodding, then slip out through the door.

The hallway is deserted, thankfully, and I make my way back to my seat in time for the third course.

Maggie leans over. "Are you okay?"

"I'm good," I answer, giving her my first genuine smile of the evening.

My sister's eyes widen. "Were you...?"

"I don't know what you're talking about."

"Ada!"

"You sound like Mother."

"Can you blame me?"

I giggle, forking the food on my plate and taking a bite without even knowing what I'm eating. It's not until I glance up to see a dark look in Count Gregory's eyes that my smile fades. I eat the rest of my meal in silence.

My eyes betray me though, drifting to the empty seat where the Duke of Blythe used to sit.

He doesn't return.

16

HEATH

A PAIR of beady black eyes see me slip out of the restroom, and a cold shot rushes down my spine. What else did those eyes see? Whoever it is disappears around a corner, and I glance down the hallway toward the dining room.

Letting out a sigh, I drop my chin to my chest.

I shouldn't be here. Count Gregory sees my presence as an act of war. He must have heard rumblings about what I'm planning. How I want to expose what he did to my brother. How I'm planning to expose every bit of fraud and misplaced philanthropy.

Last time I saw her, I got a call from the King to deliver the evidence I'd gathered against Count Gregory. I had no choice—I had to leave. No one refuses the King.

Now I know the Crown is on my side. They have investigative powers I don't possess, and I know his days are numbered.

I'll be able to destroy this man, just like he destroyed my family.

But then, there's Ada.

Dancing with him. Letting him kiss her fingers. Giving him smiles that should only belong to me.

One woman shouldn't derail my plans, but I can't help myself. Count Gregory's life is going to implode, and I don't want her to be collateral damage.

Instead of heading back to dinner, I give my apologies to the footmen at the exit and leave the building. It's the safest thing to do. It's the only way I can protect her until I can bring the full weight of the law down on Count Gregory.

But damn, it hurts. I wish I could take Ada with me and protect her from all this.

Letting my driver take me away, I stare at the dark castle behind me, hoping she'll forgive me for leaving.

17

ADA

THE MORNING after Count Gregory's dinner party, I wake up and feel so nauseous I puke, then let out a sigh and rest my head against the cool porcelain.

No gold inlay in the Belcourt toilets, by the way. Why do I feel so horrible? I didn't even drink last night.

Groaning, I check the date on my phone. Count the days since my last period. Then, I count them again.

I'm late.

My heart thumps. Panic floods my veins as I stare at my screen. I couldn't be...?

I can't even say the word. I can't even *think* the word. No. No, it's not possible. It's a stomach bug. I'm stressed about the Duke and Count Gregory and about my last piano performance this year, and I've been having more sex than usual. My hormones are all messed up.

I'm on the pill, for crying out loud!

But as I crawl up from the bathroom floor and stare at myself in the mirror, I suck in a breath. My gaze drifts to the toilet.

I puked once recently, too, just an hour or less after taking a birth control pill. Then I had unprotected sex with the Duke of Blythe.

My breath comes in short, staggered gasps. Oh my goodness. Oh no. No, no, no.

I could be pregnant with the Duke of Blythe's baby.

Squeezing my eyes shut, I turn away. I can't look at myself. This isn't happening. There's some other explanation. Food poisoning. A virus. A bug. My period will start as soon as I calm down. It has to.

My phone buzzes.

Heath: Morning, beautiful.

Any other day, that text would send a thrill of excitement coursing through my veins. He's not ignoring me. He heard me last night, and he's showing me he wants to talk to me.

Now, though?

Terror. Cold, black fear.

I type back a quick *good morning* and stuff my phone in my pocket, slipping a baggy hoodie over my head and grabbing the biggest sunglasses I own. I slip down the back stairs and get in my car, driving to a pharmacy clear across town. I don't want to be recognized.

I buy four pregnancy tests and enough chocolate to deal with the fallout of either result. If it's negative... Wait—do I *want* it to be positive? My head is a mess. I want to cry and scream and call Heath and also never speak of this to anyone, ever.

When I get home, Maggie sees me enter with a bag clutched to my chest. She frowns. "What's that? Where did you go this morning?"

"Nowhere." I turn my back to her, hurrying up the stairs.

When I get to my room and go to my en-suite bathroom, I hear my sister struggling up the stairs with her big air cast on. "Ada!"

I crack my bathroom door a fraction of an inch, seeing her standing there with her arms crossed. Sighing, I open the door wider.

Her eyes flick from me to the pregnancy tests on the vanity, and a gasp falls through her lips. "You're...?"

"I don't know. Haven't taken it yet."

"Holy shit, Ada."

I stare at my sister, biting my lip. If my prim and proper older sister is swearing, things are bad. I jerk my head to the test and she nods, understanding I'm going to take one.

I follow the instructions that come with the test, then set a timer and open the bathroom door.

Maggie sits on the edge of the bathtub with her hands propped under her chin. When my timer goes off, her eyes flick to mine.

Shaking my head, I inhale sharply. "I can't look. You do it."

Maggie gets up, putting all her weight on her good leg to lean over and grab the test. She flips it over, her eyes widening.

Shit. Fuck. Oh no, no, no.

Maggie's eyebrows arch, and she nods. "Positive."

"No."

She lets out a sigh.

I shake my head. "No. I'll take another one. It's a false positive. Has to be."

My sister places the test on the counter, nodding, and steps out of the bathroom. We do the whole thing all over again, with the same results. Then again. And again.

Positive, positive, positive.

I stare at the wall, not understanding.

I'm pregnant.

It's not until Maggie wraps her arms around me and

holds me close that I break down and cry. She shushes me, rocking back and forth as I fall apart.

But even through my tears, there's something else. A feeling that grows stronger with every passing second. I'm going to be a *mother*. There's a child growing inside me, and I'm responsible for it. Me.

Past my fear, behind my panic, there's another feeling. Love that I've never felt before. Deeper than I've ever experienced. I run my hand over my stomach, already feeling attached to the tiny fetus inside me.

My phone dings again, and we both see the Duke's name flash.

Maggie glances at me. "Are you going to tell him?"

"I don't know," I whisper, as if he'll hear me through the phone. "I don't know what to do. I don't know how I feel. I think... I think I'm happy about it." My eyes widen as I stare at my sister. "But if he's not..."

She squeezes my arms, nodding. "Take your time, Ada. You don't have to tell him right away. Just think about your options. About everything."

I nod, my heart racing—but even as I stand there, the feeling gets stronger. Love. Devotion. Absolute and total adoration. There's a baby growing inside me. Holy shit. Oh my goodness. I don't... I can't...

Whoa.

I let out a long sigh, shaking my head. "He's coming to the concert on Friday. I'll tell him I need to talk to him then. I don't want to text him about this."

Maggie nods. "Good idea. It'll give you a few days to think about how you want to tell him and what you want to do."

"I already know what I want to do," I say, straightening my shoulders. "I want to keep it."

Maggie takes a deep breath. She nods. "Okay."

By the set of her shoulders, I know I'm heaping another problem onto her back. Her wedding to Count Gregory was already important for Kiera. Now, I'll be unmarried and pregnant, which will be another blow to the Belcourt name. There's more riding on her marriage than ever before.

But my sister just gives me a hug, a smile, and tells me she's here for me no matter what.

As my concert approaches, my nerves heighten. I'll be seeing Heath for the first time since the Count's dinner party. He'll be watching me play. Afterward, I'm hoping to sit him down and tell him the truth.

My stomach is tied up in knots as I wait just offstage. But I close my eyes and think of the music, and it slows my heart enough for me to be able to walk out with my head held high. With the bright stage lights shining down on me, I can't see any individual faces in the crowd, and I'm grateful for it.

I settle onto the piano bench and take a deep breath, and I play.

The crowd melts away. My fears about the future melt away. The thought of the Duke and the Count and my family —all gone.

For a few blissful moments, I'm at peace. I play for an hour, feeling lighter and happier than I have in weeks. In a way, I feel like this concert belongs to me and my baby. We're united on this stage. My little secret. My child, growing inside my womb.

For now, at least, no one knows. There's no controversy. No difficult conversations. Only love—and music.

Then the concert ends, I take a bow, and I walk offstage. When I see the Duke of Blythe waiting in the wings for me, my heart flips. A smile tugs at my lips, and I know things between us are special.

He's here, just like he said he'd be. Even though I've been distant since I took the test. Even though I told him I wanted to speak to him about something important. Even though my sister will be marrying Count Gregory.

This could work. Maybe he'll see the glow on my face and know that this baby is special. Our connection, as short as it has been, means something.

I take a step toward him, but my mother blocks my path.

"Ada," she says, putting a hand on my arm, "I need to speak to you."

"One moment, Mother," I say, trying to pull away.

Heath takes a step closer to us, his eyes shining. Does he know I played that concert for our child? I played it in honor of the feelings already in full bloom inside me.

"Ada," my mother snaps.

I frown. "Is everything all right?"

"Count Gregory is here," she hisses.

"Okay." I shrug, but she still won't let go. My mother's eyes are dark. She gulps, and dread crawls up my spine. "What is it, Mother?"

"The Count spoke to me when you finished playing," she says. "He doesn't want to marry Maggie."

I let out a sigh. "Thank God. I never liked him."

Her brows draw together. "No, Ada..." Her grip on my arm tightens. I steal a glance at Heath, panic pushing in at the edges of my consciousness. My mother sucks in a breath. "Ada, Count Gregory wants you instead."

My ears ring. Eyes widen. I'm dizzy.

"W-What?" I grip the wall, eyes searching for the Duke. Horror writes itself over his features as I try to gulp past a lump in my throat. I inhale, shaking my head. "No."

"Ada," my mother says. "Think of Kiera."

"No, we can... Loans. Scholarships. We... I don't..."

I inhale hard. Then again. Then again. I'm hyperventilating. I can't get enough air. I can't make words. The world is spinning. Why is my vision blurry?

I can't marry the Count. I don't want Maggie to marry him, but I definitely don't want it to be me. I open my eyes again, trying to focus on the Duke. He's still standing just at the edges of the shadows.

Then, his face comes into sharp focus.

Deep, dark rage.

He's angry.

My brows draw together and I try to reach for him, but another hand slips into mine.

"Dearest Ada," the Count croaks, blocking my view of the Duke. "I hope you'll forgive me for my rudeness. I just couldn't go on thinking of anyone else." His beady black eyes rake over me, and it hurts. Physically. Mentally.

I can't think. Can't breathe. I pull my hand away. "Excuse me."

I stumble away, searching frantically for the Duke, even though I already know he's gone.

18

HEATH

COUNT GREGORY WANTS to marry Ada.

This is an attack. It's directed at me. I know it is. He saw me and Ada together at his Christmas party, and he decided to step in and take her from me, too. Just like he took everything else.

Whoever saw me exiting the bathroom must have whispered into his ear, and now his poisonous tentacles are reaching back into my life.

I feel sick.

I need to talk to her.

But what will I say?

I left the concert hall without saying a word to her, even though I could see the agony on her face. She doesn't want to marry him—but I know what it means to her family.

The Count knows every dean at every major university on the continent. He can offer stability for their family and a good education for Ada's little sister.

What can I offer? What do I have?

A knock sounds on my office door, and I call out for the visitor to enter.

My personal butler, Seville, steps in. "Lady Belcourt is here, Your Grace. She's waiting in the formal living room."

I hide my shock behind a stone façade. "Thank you. I'll be right there."

Seville bows and exits the office, closing the door softly as he goes.

I stare at the closed door, my heart banging against my chest.

She's here. She came straight here. That's good, right? That means she feels something for me? It means she wants to refuse the Count?

On trembling legs, I stand up. I take a deep breath and stare at the door, willing myself to take a step forward.

What if she's here to break it to me gently? She wants me to hear of the betrothal from her own lips, and tell me she doesn't want to see me anymore? What if this is the end?

It can't be the end. It *can't.* I can't allow her to marry the Count when I'm so close to bringing charges against him. We almost have enough evidence to bring a case against him. I just need one more university to release their documents to the royal investigators, and we'll have enough to put the Count away for good. He'll rot in jail, exactly where he deserves to be.

But if she marries him...that will ruin her, too. It'll bring shame on her whole family.

Can I do that to her?

Steeling myself against whatever Ada has to say, I take the first step. Then another. Soon I'm standing outside the formal living room, peering in.

God, she's gorgeous. The weak winter sun streams in through the window and makes her black hair glow. Her skin looks like it's made of porcelain, her soft features turned toward the window. All I want to do is run my hands over her waist and pull her close, burying my face in her hair once more.

I shouldn't have run away from the concert hall. She's still wearing her dress, a black slip that made her look like a goddess on stage.

When I clear my throat, she turns. Anguish is painted across her features, and my stomach knots.

She's not here to tell me she's refusing the Count. She's not here to profess her undying love. Why would she? We've only known each other for a couple of weeks.

She's here to break it to me in person. Pain lashes across my chest, leaving deep welts across my skin. I grind my teeth to stop from wincing.

"Lady Belcourt," I say through a clenched jaw.

"Heath," she sighs, taking a step toward me. She stops, her brows drawing together. A hand goes to her stomach as her chest heaves, and she watches me. Reads my features. Tries to understand.

"I heard the Count's proposal," I say after a long silence.

Ada doesn't answer. She stares at me, a thousand emotions flitting across her face.

So I stand rooted to the ground, letting the familiar sting of agony course through my veins. My lips turn down. "Are you here to break it to me gently? To tell me that you can't see me anymore?"

"No, I—" She stops, sucking in a breath. A flash of pain crosses her eyes.

I shrug. "He's not a good man, Ada. You should refuse."

Her breath trembles as her shoulders round. "Heath, it's for my sister. We can't afford to send her to university, and the Count, he—"

"Has connections at every major university you can think of," I finish, chuckling bitterly. I want to cross the distance between us and wrap my arms around her. I want to drop to my knees and tell her to marry me instead.

But I don't.

If I do that, what can I offer her? I don't have the connections the Count has. I can't offer her sister entrance to any university she chooses. I can't elevate her family's standing in society. If anything, being with me would drag her down.

Of course the Count has something I can't give. Of course a betrothal to him is more attractive than I could ever be. He took everything from me, why would Ada be any different?

As soon as my brother died, I knew my life would change forever. I just didn't expect to feel this kind of pain all over again. This time, I'm losing someone I never even had in the first place.

I lift my eyes to hers. "Is this what you want?"

Ada's eyes scream. Lips drop open. She shakes her head, then lets out a heavy sigh. "No. But..." When my black-haired beauty lifts her eyes to mine again, my heart clenches. Cracks split across its surface, sending pain radiating through my chest.

This hurts more than anything. My feelings for her are stronger than I realized, but she's being snatched away from me before I had a chance to admit it.

But what can I do? I can't give her what her family needs. As I stand there, realizing the true depths of my feelings for Ada, I almost want to laugh.

If she marries the Count, I have to stop my investigations. I can't bring any charges against him. I can't avenge my brother. I can't clear my family's name. I can't fulfill my last promise to my parents by showing the world what a monster Count Gregory really is.

I can't do any of that, because if I go after the Count, I'll hurt Ada.

Is this why he's marrying her? Because he knows how close the police are to being able to charge him with a litany of crimes? He knows I'm dying to stand before him in the witness box, gloating?

Now, I can't. Clever monster. He's using the only protection I can't break through.

Ada.

I give her a curt nod. "I understand."

"Heath—"

"Do you need someone to drive you home?"

Her lips snap shut, an unreadable expression in her eyes. Ada's throat clenches, as if she struggles to swallow. She shakes her head. "That won't be necessary," she answers in a tight voice.

"Good. Well, congratulations." I give her my back and walk out, catching one final glimpse of her crumpling face.

I've lost everything.

My brother, my parents, the family business, the honor of our name. All I have is a big, empty castle and a loyal staff, but no one to share it with. No little dukes and duchesses to fill these halls with laughter. No future. No wife.

No love.

The Count took everything from me, and now he's taking the last hope I ever had at love.

19

ADA

WHY DID I COME HERE? What did I expect? For the Duke of Blythe to fall to his knees and beg me to marry him instead? To tell him about the baby and expect him to be filled with joy?

Ha.

Ridiculous.

It takes every ounce of power and pride within me to hold myself together as I'm led back out of the expansive castle and to my vehicle. A footman holds the door open for me, the ignition already started and heat turned up to a comfortable temperature. I slip into the driver's seat and nod to the footman before backing out of the garage.

I make it down the long driveway and through the gate before I have to pull over to sob.

He wouldn't even listen. Wouldn't even let me speak. How was I supposed to tell him about the baby? The Duke's face was shuttered. Closed off. Unreachable.

He thought I wanted the Count. Thought I had already accepted the proposal.

And now?

I can't go back there. I can't tell him about the baby now that he's tossed me aside like a used tissue.

I'm on my own.

Even if I march back there and tell him about the baby, can I handle a rejection? Can I withstand the assault of his cold, hostile eyes?

I swear he thinks less of me for considering a marriage to the Count, but what choice do I have? Unless some other eligible bachelor begs one of us to marry them, I have to accept the Count's proposal.

Eligible bachelors aren't exactly in great supply.

A dagger embeds itself in my chest as my heart breaks. It was naive of me to come here and think the Duke would save me. He wanted me when I was pliable and available. When I could distract him at boring parties. When I could be the one to sneak off with him for a bit of fun.

But now, when the reality of our lives comes into sharp focus?

He turns his back on me and walks out.

We've known each other for three weeks. How could that possibly lead to anything real? How could I think it would end well?

Stupid, silly girl.

I cry, my forehead resting on my steering wheel. Then a wave of nausea makes me open the car door and throw up all over the ground. Lovely. How very regal of me. I let out a dry laugh, staring up at the dark sky and wishing it would fall down on top of me.

With a sigh, I'm able to gather myself up again. I close the door, wipe my eyes on the back of my hand, and take a deep, clearing breath. Then, I put the car in gear.

When I get home, Maggie is waiting for me. She wraps

me in a tight hug, letting her own tears soak into my shirt. I know she wants to take my pain away, but she can't.

"I'm so sorry, Ada. I wish it were still me."

I pull back, taking a deep breath. "I have to tell the Count about the baby."

"You're going to keep it?" she asks, eyebrows arching.

I grind my teeth. "Yes." My eyes flash, daring her to protest. Shame smarts my skin as I gulp down my fear. I nod. "I'm keeping it. It's the only thing that feels good right now."

"And the Duke?"

I take a deep breath, remembering the chill in his voice. I shake my head. "Our relationship wasn't what I thought it was."

Maggie bites the inside of her cheek, her brows drawing together. She drops her hand to mine, squeezing gently. "I'm proud of you, Ada."

"For getting knocked up?"

"For staying true to yourself." She wraps me in another hug, pulling back to look me in the eye. "When you tell the Count about the baby, tell him that I'm still willing to marry him if your pregnancy is a dealbreaker."

"Even though he refused you for me? Maggie—"

"I'll do it," my sister says, nodding once. She gives me a tight hug, but I don't think she realizes how much it means to me.

Even though I'm pregnant with another man's child. Even though her supposed future fiancé rejected her for me. Even though I've been irresponsible and silly and naive, she's still right here beside me. Ready to take the load on her shoulders. Ready to give up her life and happiness for me. For the family.

I don't deserve her.

. . .

THE NEXT DAY I find myself standing in another man's living room, staring out a different window at a very similar landscape. A few fresh inches of snow fell overnight, the glittering blanket of white almost blinding in the midday sun.

A sound behind me makes me turn. I give Count Gregory a small curtsy, bowing my head. My expression remains neutral.

Ever since my visit with the Duke of Blythe, it feels like my emotions have been locked away somewhere deep. The Count's dark eyes stare at me over his long nose, but his gaze doesn't make me feel sick. There's no prickling of the hair on the back of my neck, or slithering disgust crawling down my spine.

Just...nothing. I'm empty.

When I straighten up again, the Count gestures to a small bar at the side of the room. "Drink?"

I shake my head, resisting the urge to put a hand to my stomach. Ever since I took those pregnancy tests, it's like a protective instinct has flared inside me. I'm constantly touching my stomach, shielding it from anything and everything.

Today, though, I force myself to stand tall.

Count Gregory pours himself a drink, a big ice cube clinking against the crystal glass. He raises it to his lips, watching me over the rim. "I wasn't expecting to see you today," he says, gesturing to a long sofa. "Your mother told me you were ill last night."

I perch myself on the edge of the couch, nodding. "Yes. I apologize for my...hasty exit."

"You're here to tell me your answer to my proposal."

"I am."

The Count sits opposite me, leaning back on the sofa and crossing his legs. He looks completely at ease, comfortable in the knowledge that he's in control. He's blessed me with a proposal, and I'm here to show my gratitude.

Isn't that what this is? I should kiss his feet for helping my poor family.

The only hurdle is the baby growing inside me.

I take a deep breath, straightening my spine. I clasp my hands on my lap, lifting my eyes to his. "Before we go any further, there's something I need to tell you."

The Count's body stays completely relaxed. He doesn't move at all, except for an almost imperceptible twitch of his eyebrow.

Blood pumps hard through my veins, and fear arcs up inside me. I know I need to tell him. I can't marry him without him knowing I'm carrying another man's child.

But—this could ruin everything. I've already lost the Duke, and now I'll ruin my family's future, too.

Shoving those thoughts down inside me, I take a deep breath. "I'm pregnant."

The Count stiffens, not quite able to hide his surprise. His legs uncross, a foot hitting the ground with a thud. He leans forward, opening his mouth, then pauses. His glass of amber alcohol touches his lips, and he takes a deep gulp.

Silence stretches longer. I look away.

My cheeks redden, and I try to push aside the shame. I shouldn't be ashamed. This is the twenty-first century, and I'm a grown woman. People get pregnant all the time. If my family's situation was any different, I would feel nothing but joy. I'm sure of it.

Count Gregory watches me, leaning forward. His face is impassive. The way his lips pinch makes me think he's angry, but he hides it well. His eyes darken, dropping down the length of my body.

Finally, he speaks. "Who..." A sharp intake of breath.

Understanding washes over his features. Then, a cruel, victorious smile. "Blythe."

I gulp. "The father isn't important," I say, using all my years of training to keep my face flat and my voice strong. "I merely wanted to tell you before we take this any further. Maggie is still—"

"I don't want Maggie," the Count says, waving a hand.

I frown.

His smile widens. Dipping his chin down toward me, the Count lets out a low chuckle. His eyes flash, and a sense of dread twists my stomach. The Count puts his crystal tumbler down on a side table, wiping his hands on a thick white napkin. He nods. "I'll raise the child as my own. We can marry soon to avoid questions. Christmas Eve? I've always liked the thought of a Christmas wedding."

"I don't—" I stop, not even sure what I was going to say.

Christmas Eve is only a few days away. He wants to marry me within *days*.

My mask falls, and I frown. "You still want me?"

"My darling Ada," he croons, standing up and reaching for my hand. "I've wanted you since the moment I laid eyes on you."

When my palm slips against his, nausea makes my head spin. This isn't what I expected. I thought he'd be angry. I thought maybe he'd take Maggie instead. I thought I might be shamed, cast out of polite society.

But the Count...he still wants to marry me? He'll accept this child? This isn't some sick ruse?

Confusion freezes my limbs, and I let the Count wrap his arms around my waist. He drops a cold kiss on my cheek, then grabs my chin in his hand. I wince. He's gripping my face so tight it'll leave a mark, his other hand clamped around my back.

When his lips dip down to mine, I pinch them closed and try to push away. He lets his lips cover mine, the stench of mothballs making me want to retch. His lips are cold and hard against mine. I struggle, letting out a whimper.

The Count releases me, laughing. *Laughing.* At me. At my struggle. At my predicament. At my complete and utter powerlessness. "I'll make arrangements. We'll marry on Christmas Eve." He throws me a cruel look. "That should save the tatters of your reputation."

And with that, Count Gregory turns and walks out, and my world shatters.

20

ADA

WHITE DRESS. Veil. Makeup. Hair.

I look like a bride.

I feel like dirt.

Kiera fluffs the hem of my dress, smiling up at me from the floor. "You look beautiful, Ada. I can't believe you're getting married. Only a month ago, you were going to the Christmas ball!"

I smooth my hands over the lacy dress, sucking a breath in through my teeth. "I know. I can't believe it, either."

"And on Christmas Eve, too! It would be romantic if—" She stops herself, biting her lip. "I mean, it *is* romantic."

I let out a humorless laugh. "You mean it would be romantic if I were marrying anyone else?"

She stands up, shifting her weight from foot to foot. "I didn't say that."

"It's okay." I spread my arms, giving my little sister a hug. The door opens behind us, and Maggie steps through. She gulps at the sight of me, wrestling her lips into a weak smile. Wrapping her arms around the two of us, my sisters and I stand in a silent hug.

This isn't where I thought I'd be just a month after the Christmas ball at Farcliff Castle. I never should have gone. I wouldn't be pregnant or engaged or feeling like my life was ending.

But here I am.

What choice do I have? If I don't marry the Count, I'm not only securing a fall from grace for myself, but I'm basically ensuring that my entire family will follow. I'd be stopping Kiera's higher education and failing to provide stability for my parents.

I have to do this.

But as I stare at myself in the mirror, dropping my gaze to my still-flat stomach, my heart clenches. I'm carrying the Duke of Blythe's child, but he'll never know. He'll see me bear a child with the Count. Maybe he'll imagine me in bed with Count Gregory, desecrating the memories we created together.

I squeeze my eyes shut. The thought of Count Gregory touching me anywhere—let alone down there—makes me want to throw up.

But this is what I have to do. It's what my family needs. It's what my child deserves—a stable upbringing without the disapproving whispers of society. Without the shame.

A knock on the door signals that it's time to go down to the main hall. We're in Count Gregory's mansion, in a room in the east wing.

I turn to the door, nodding to Maggie. She opens it up, greeting the footman on the other side. My sisters and I exchange one last glance, then start walking. It's a slow, somber procession through the shadowy halls of the Gregory Castle.

My new home.

This place has none of the warmth and lightness of the

Duke's estate. None of the family photos and easy comfort. None of the love. It's cold and lifeless. Dread snakes through my chest, emotion crushing my ribs so tight I can't breathe.

Our footsteps echo in the silence, until we round a corner and hear the faint music of the classic wedding processional song. Each note hammers another nail in my coffin, and I blink back tears.

I need to do this. I need to do this. I need to do this.

It's for my family. My sisters. My parents. My child.

I need to do this.

It's a mantra, repeated with every step. But as we get closer to the chapel, my stomach clenches. Every instinct tells me to run. The arched doorway leading to the chapel opens like a wide maw, waiting to swallow me whole.

I shiver.

My mother exits the chapel, nodding. This is it. In minutes, I'll be a married woman. My honor will be saved, and my family's future will be secure.

So why does it feel so awful?

I pause outside the chapel, letting my sisters walk ahead. I hear the shuffling of fabric, like a small crowd of people turning to watch their entrance. Closing my eyes, I swallow my emotion. I'm next.

One step forward, and I cross the threshold. Another, and I'm in the aisle. A third, and the Count comes into view.

His thin lips are curled into a mean smile, his narrow, dark eyes dropping down the length of my body. There's a dirty, possessive look on his face. And something else glittering in his eyes.

Triumph. Like he's won a prize.

I feel sick.

I take one more step, my bottom lip trembling. I know I should hide it. I know I should pretend to be happy—but why? My family knows I don't want this. The only other guests are a few witnesses for the Count, and a few members of his staff. Who cares if I cry?

The Count's smile widens, darkness unfurling across his features. He *likes* my suffering.

Then, his smile freezes. The edges of his lips drop a fraction of an inch, and I hear shouting behind me. The four-piece string orchestra falters, playing a few discordant notes before stopping.

I pause, turning to look behind me.

My eyes widen, a tear finally spilling down my cheek.

A dozen uniformed police officers are rushing down the hall, followed by two men in suits and—

Oh my goodness. The Duke. He's here.

He's *here*.

I freeze, letting the police officers rush past me, followed by men with royal crests on their uniforms. From the palace? Their dirty, snow-covered boots stomp all over the train of my dress, but I don't care. My heart hammers, watching them march right up to the altar.

One of the men trailing behind, wearing a brown suit and an oversized trench, pulls out a pair of handcuffs. "Chester Gregory, you're under arrest for fraud." He rattles off a long speech of rights as I stand there, dumbfounded.

The Count's eyes stare just past me, glued to the Duke's face. When the handcuffs click over his wrists, his trance finally breaks, and a roar rips through his throat. A ripple passes through the tiny audience as Count Gregory's face twists, his teeth snapping at anyone around.

I tremble, shrinking away from the animal in cuffs.

Then, like a warm blanket on a cold day, an arm circles my waist. The Duke pulls me back and to the side to let the procession of police officers carry a struggling Count Gregory past. Heath's arm stays wrapped around my waist as the Count spits in our direction, yelling obscenities until his voice fades down the hallway.

My breath is shallow. My head is spinning. I claw at my veil, pulling it out of my hair and tossing it to the side, trying to get enough oxygen to fill my lungs.

He's leaving. I'm not marrying him. How... Why...

I turn to look at the Duke of Blythe, my eyes wide. His stubble has grown to a beard, as if he hasn't shaved in a week. Instinctively, I run my fingers through the coarse hair, earning a soft groan of contentment from the Duke.

"What..." I inhale sharply. "Why are you here? What's going on?"

"Count Gregory tried to gloat," he says, placing a hand to my stomach. "He called me last night and told me about the baby. Said you'd agreed to marry him to save your reputation." Heath's hand sweeps up my body to cup my face, warm and strong and safe. "Ada, I'm so sorry. Your visit made sense. I'm sorry I didn't let you speak. I should have listened. I thought..." His eyebrows draw together. "I thought you were choosing him. That he could provide things I never could. That your future would be better if you married the Count."

I shake my head. "No." It's all I can manage to say. My voice is hoarse.

"I've been working on bringing him down for years," Heath says, his brows arching. He closes his eyes, letting out a long breath. "He funded the research for an experimental drug that killed my brother. It was supposed to be a miracle drug that cured addiction. They told us early clinical trials had been successful. That it was safe." Heath scoffs, tears filling his eyes. "My brother's heart stopped after the very first dose."

"Heath," I whisper. "I had no idea."

"No one did. It was covered up, and I was never able to prove it. Just another dead junkie, you know? But I knew it was him. He's a major investor in almost every pharmaceutical company on the continent."

My eyes widen. "It's not just philanthropy and medical research."

Heath shakes his head. "It's why he's so well-connected to research institutions and universities." His lips pinch. "He killed my brother. Just months later, my parents died. They couldn't handle the shame and heartbreak, and I think it just broke them. He took everything from me, and I couldn't even prove it." The Duke's eyes grow hard. "I'll never forgive him. I couldn't prove what he did, but I knew if I dug deep enough, I'd find something. And I did. Fraud and embezzlement on a massive scale. He's been stealing money from almost every institution and company he's involved with."

My heart thuds. I was moments away from marrying that man. I thought I was doing right by my family, but what kind of future would I have had with him?

Running my fingers up to the Duke's shoulders, I shake my head. It feels so good to touch him. To be here with him. To feel safe for the first time in weeks. And the way he's looking at me, it makes me think that maybe there's hope. For me. For *us*. "Why didn't you tell me this earlier? Why not explain it when I came to see you?"

His thumb sweeps over my cheek, catching a stray tear. "Because I told myself your family and your future would be safer if you were tied to him. I'd drop the investigation. Let him walk."

"Heath...you'd do that? How could you think I was better off with a man like that?"

He closes his eyes, letting out a long breath. "What could I offer you? How could I help Kiera's university applications? I dropped the investigation and resigned myself to never avenging my brother." The Duke leans his head to mine, closing his eyes. "I'm sorry, Ada. I should never have let you walk out. I should have wrapped my arms around you and begged you to marry me right then. I should have told you how I feel about you."

"And how's that?" I manage to croak.

He pulls back, cupping my face. His eyes, so green, so vivid, so completely full of emotion, shine for me. "Like you're the reason I'm still alive. Like you're the only good thing that has ever happened to me."

"You don't even know me," I whisper, knowing it's a lie. From the moment I saw him across the room, we understood each other. Our connection is more than physical. It's deep, and true, and eternal.

"I know you deserve better than this marriage. I know you're carrying my child. I know I could never live with myself if you took any other man's name but my own."

"What if I want to keep my own name?" I whisper, letting my lips slide into a smile.

"Fine," Heath says, grinning. "Just as long as you're mine."

And with that, Heath crushes his lips to mine. He kisses me in front of my family. In front of the priest and the scandalized staff of the Gregory household. In front of the whole world.

I wrap my arms around his neck and let my heart sing.

This. This is where I want to be. This is where the world feels right.

In the Duke's arms. By his side. Promised to no one else but him.

EPILOGUE

HEATH

ADA INVITES me back to the Belcourt Estate, her family graciously echoing the invitation. As we arrive, a soft sprinkling of snow starts to fall.

Ada glances at me from the passenger seat of my car, reaching over to slide her hand over my thigh. "This isn't what I expected for Christmas this year."

I grin. "Me neither."

I park the car, pausing as I watch the rest of her family filter inside. Ada smiles shyly. And I can't resist. I have to kiss her. I tangle my fingers into those black locks and take her lips in mine. She tastes like heaven and hope and everything good in the world.

Right there, in the car, after breaking up her wedding and leading the police to the Count's residence, I vow to never let her go.

It doesn't matter that we barely know each other. It doesn't matter that we've started a relationship with furtive kisses and stolen passions.

I feel more alive than I have in years. It feels like my brother and parents are smiling down on me, watching me mend the wounds that were inflicted upon me years before. Ada is the healing balm. With soft lips and moans that slip through our kiss, she holds me tight and stitches me back together.

When we pull apart, Ada stares at the Count's engagement ring on her left hand. Tugging the simple gold band free, she shakes her head. "Wearing that thing felt wrong from the beginning."

"I should have given you one the day you came to see me," I say, my voice a low rasp. "When you played my mother's piano. I should have dropped to my knees and begged you to marry me."

Patting my chest, I find the little black velvet box containing my mother's old ring. Before she died, she made me promise to give it to someone. She told me not to let bitterness and anger cloud the rest of my life. She told me to fall in love, and to fall hard.

For the first time, I feel like I've fulfilled that vow.

I pull out the box, flipping it open and lifting my eyes to Ada. "I know I'm an idiot for letting you walk away from me. I know I've ignored you and kept the truth of my investigation from you. I know you have every right to refuse me, but I'm not afraid to beg. Ada Belcourt, meeting you was like being struck by lightning. You've lit up my entire world, and it's only in the past four weeks that I've realized how dark life is without you."

She stares at the glittering stone, flicking her eyes up to mine. "This is not how I expected tonight to go at all."

A thin blanket of snow is already covering the vehicle, shielding us from prying eyes. It feels warm and secure in here, like we're alone in the world. I gulp, tugging the ring free from its velvet box.

"Marry me, Ada." My hand is shaking. Breath short. Eyes moist.

Everything I have, Ada holds in the palm of her hand. She has my heart, my future, my child. If she refuses me, I know I'll never recover.

With a thick gulp, Ada nods. "Okay."

I smile so hard it hurts my cheeks. My chest feels like it's cracked open. *Okay* means yes. *Okay* means she's mine, now and forever.

As I slip the ring on her finger, she lets out a hiccup and a laugh, shaking her head. "It fits."

"Meant to be." My eyes shine with unshed tears as I smile at my future bride. We were destined to find each other. From the moment I first saw her, she was meant to be my wife.

Sliding her hand over my cheek, Ada lets out a sigh. "Merry Christmas, Your Grace." She grins at the title. "Heath," she corrects.

"Merry Christmas," I answer, leaning into her touch. Words stick to my throat, but I want to tell her. I need to tell her. I'm sick of hiding in my mansion, away from the stares and the whispers and the emotions. I'm sick of living my life in fear, focused only on revenge.

Ada has shown me another side of life.

"I love you," I whisper, placing my palm on her thigh. "I never believed in love at first sight until I saw you. And when I heard you play that piano at the Farcliff Castle, I knew my life would never be the same. You've reached into my chest and pulled my heart free of the thorns caging it in. You've awoken feelings inside me that I didn't know were possible." I take a deep breath, closing my eyes as her fingers stroke my cheek. "And you're carrying my child. I thought"—I pause, forcing my eyes open—"that I'd never have an heir. I thought my family would die with me. But..."

My voice drifts off, and I slide my hand from her thigh to her abdomen.

With one hand still cupping my face, Ada places a palm over my hand on her stomach, intertwining my fingers with mine. "You want the baby?" she whispers, hope blooming over her face.

"Want it?" I laugh. "Ada, I'm desperate for it. Desperate for you. Did you hear me? I love you. Completely. I never want to let you go. I never want to watch you walk away from me again."

"Technically, you walked away from me." She grins, squeezing my hand. Then, biting her lip, she blinks two tears free from her eyes. "I think I might love you, too."

Our story is messy. It's backwards. It's fast and tangled and not at all what I would have expected. But in Ada's eyes I see the truth, even if her words are hesitant.

She loves me. She *loves* me. The mother of my child, my future wife, the woman who dragged me out of the bitterness of my own past—she loves me. Me! How did I ever deserve this? How could I have gained not only a wife, but a child, too?

Leaning over to lay a kiss on my lips, Ada smiles. "Come on," she says. "We do presents on Christmas Eve at my house. I'm sure my mother will have rustled something up for you, too."

"You're my gift this year," I say, letting a smile stretch over my lips. My heart thumps hard, reminding me that I'm alive. That I have a future with Ada. That I have a child on the way, and I'll do everything in my power to provide for my baby. *Our* baby.

. . .

I SPEND Christmas with the Belcourts, then marry Ada a week later. We spend every single day together, walking through snow-covered fields and admiring the crisp, blue skies that seem even bluer in the cold weather. I kiss her often, telling her I love her multiple times a day. How could I not? I never thought I'd feel this way. I never thought I'd have this.

A wife. A family.

Happiness.

I don't stay stuck at the Blythe Estate anymore. I go to every concert that Ada puts on. We go to the theatre and the ballet. We go see movies. We become fixtures in the tabloids, which makes Ada laugh.

"They don't need to explain my relation to the royal family anymore." She giggles, pointing to the newspaper. She looks cute with her cheeks tinged pink from the cold weather and her eyes shining bright. I kiss the tip of her nose.

As our child grows inside her, so too does my love for her bloom. If I thought this was just a passing attraction, I'm proven wrong every single day. Whenever I wake up with my wife's arm slung across my chest, or I get to kiss her soft lips and feel her swelling belly under my palm, I know this is real. It's deep. It's everlasting.

Our son is born the first week of September, exactly forty weeks after that fateful Christmas ball, on a particularly warm autumn day. Ada is gorgeous and strong and I fall in love with her all over again. The past nine months have shown me what it means to live.

We name him Paul, after my brother. He's perfect.

THE CASE against Count Gregory is strong, and he's sentenced to sixty years in prison on multiple counts of fraud and embezzlement. His crimes turn out to be so egregious that the judge uses him as an example, giving a damning speech at the sentencing hearing. It makes waves around the world, with his sneering face plastered on the front page of every major newspaper.

Truth be told, Gregory's conviction has little impact on the pharmaceutical companies and research institutions that developed harmful drugs with him, but I decide his punishment is a good enough start. Fighting against unsafe drugs will be my crusade, and I'll fight it gladly—as long as Ada is by my side.

After all, if not for Gregory I might not have had the courage to shed my fears and pursue love. Pursue Ada. I would have let her slip through my fingers and I'd have stayed tucked away in my own estate, cursing the world.

Our next Christmas is spent at the Belcourt Estate. Kiera ends up attending Farcliff University, studying medicine. Maggie's foot heals, and she continues dancing. Their parents accept me with open arms, and I finally feel like I have a family again.

With a four-month-old baby in her arms, Ada sits next to the big Christmas tree in the Belcourt living room, looking like a goddess. She picks up a small envelope and hands it to me, smiling. "Merry Christmas, my love."

I tilt my head, staring at her curiously.

She smiles, nodding for me to open the envelope as she bounces baby Paul in one arm. Is it wrong that I think she looks hot right now?

Tearing my eyes away from my wife, I open the envelope and pull out an invoice. Frowning, I read it, recognizing my parents' piano-making business letterhead. "What's this?"

"I made inquiries," Ada says, smiling. "All the craftsmen

who worked for your parents missed making Blythe pianos. They all agreed to come back, and one of them even knew an old client who wanted a new instrument." She nods to the invoice. "That's the first order for the second generation of Blythe pianos."

My throat grows tight. Eyes mist. I can't even see Ada clearly now, only a vague form of her rocking our child in her arms. "You... Is this real? They want to come back?"

"Everyone read the news, Heath," she says softly, coming to sit beside me. "They all wanted to stand by you. They know you respect the business, and the only reason you shut it down was to pursue the investigation against Gregory. But that's over now." She nudges her shoulder against mine. "We can move on. Together."

Wiping my eyes with the heels of my palms, I shake my head. "Ada..." Emotion chokes me. When my vision clears, I see her smiling at me, and my heart erupts.

"I love you," I say, kissing her. "So much."

"Okay, okay!" Kiera shouts from across the room. "Get a room or hand out another Christmas present to someone else. I don't want to watch a make-out session."

Giggling, Ada pulls away. I throw my arm over her shoulders, letting out a deep breath. In this room, with Ada, our son, and my new family, I know I have everything I'll ever need.

Ada leans her head on my shoulder, and I kiss her temple. My love. My Ada. Forever.

∽

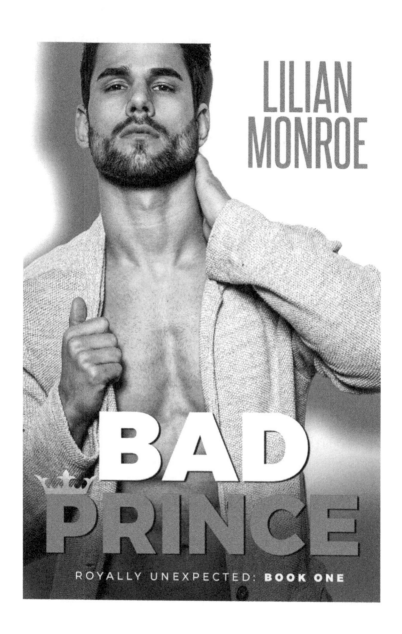

BAD PRINCE

ROYALLY UNEXPECTED: BOOK ONE

LILIAN MONROE

BAD PRINCE

ROYALLY UNEXPECTED: BOOK 1

1

ELLE

THE RHYTHMIC SQUEAKING of my housemate's bedsprings gets louder as the sound of her first moan floats through the wall. I stuff my earplugs in deeper, hoping they'll help block out the noise—even though I already know they won't. Dahlia's headboard taps against our shared wall. It starts gently, barely grazing the thin separation between our bedrooms.

And then it gets louder, and louder, and louder...

... until the wall actually *shakes*.

Another moan sounds out and a man says something barely audible. I assume it's something filthy. Dahlia, my best and weirdest friend, likes it dirty.

Why do I know this?

Because I hear everything in this rundown, mouse-infested house of ours.

Everything.

Groaning, I turn to my side, stuffing my pillow over my head to try to muffle the noise. I check the time on my phone. It's already past midnight, and I have to be up in four hours for crew practice. I'm going to be out on the water, rowing my little heart out as I train for the biggest regatta of my life, with less than four hours' sleep.

Sunday is—or rather, *was*— my day off, as usual, and Monday practices are notoriously tough after a rest day. Coach Bernard doesn't tolerate lateness, sleepiness, or excuses like *my roommate is a sex maniac.*

The banging on the wall continues, and my blood pressure rises. Every knock on the wall cranks my nerves tighter.

Bang. Bang. Bang.

Moan.

Bang. Bang. Bang.

Moan.

Dahlia goes to Farcliff University, too, but she's far from athletic—well, not in the traditional sense of the word. She runs her own athletics department from the comfort of her own bed.

No, Dahlia doesn't need to wake up at four o'clock in the morning, or practice twice a day, six days a week. She doesn't need to manage her protein intake down to the gram, or make sure her performance is stellar every single day just to keep her scholarship.

Unlike me, Dahlia can have manic, crazy sex every night of the week until the sun comes up...

... and she does.

When her voice goes up a couple octaves and a scream finally pierces the partition, I've had enough. My frustration boils over and I clamber onto my knees on the bed, banging my fist against the paper-thin wall so hard my knuckles bruise.

"Come on, you idiot! Make her come already!"

The squeaking stops. The moans pause.

Silence.

Then, the bead creaks once more as their weight shifts,

and peals of laughter sound through the wall. I slump back down on my own bed, exhaling as I rub my hands over my face.

If Dahlia wasn't the friendliest person I'd ever met—and if I could afford to live somewhere other than this rodent-plagued sex den—I'd definitely move out.

Unfortunately, though, I'm stuck here.

They move to the floor, thankfully. The floorboards aren't nearly as noisy as the bed.

BLEARY-EYED AND GRUMPY, I somehow make it to practice on time. In the locker room, I pull on my thermal, skin-hugging workout tights. My sports bra has so many straps and support mechanisms that it looks like it was designed by NASA for a trip to outer space.

I strap the bra on and adjust it, locking the girls down nice and securely. When I pull on my workout top and lean over to shove my bag in my locker, I feel the chill of the air over my lower back. Clothes never fit properly over my tall, athletic body, but I'm used to it by now.

I used to hate my height when I was a kid. As a teenager, I'd see all the boys going gaga over petite, delicate little waifs —and I felt like an ogre in comparison. Then I grew these massive knockers and I hated them, too, because all the boys went gaga over my boobs and forgot that there was a person attached to them.

I've always been taller, broader, and stronger than most men. My size isn't great for my love life, if I'm honest—I get friend zoned more often than I'd like to admit.

But my height means I can row. When I'm rowing, my breasts can be strapped down and kept out of the way. My rowing scholarship allows me to attend Farcliff University, where I'll hopefully make something of myself—and I wouldn't trade that opportunity for anything. With just over a year left until I graduate, I can honestly say that rowing has been my ticket out of a shitty, dead-end Grimdale life.

Would I like a gaggle of boyfriends to follow me around like a parade of little ducklings? Sure—why not? But am I going to stop rowing to get them?

Hell no.

Someone opens the locker room door and a blast of cold air whips through the room. I shiver, but I know as soon as I get out onto the water and start rowing, I'll be warm.

Then, a nasally, pretentious voice pierces my ears. My lips turn downward.

"Did you get your invitation yet?" Olivia Brundle's falsetto voice makes my stomach turn. I was hoping I wouldn't have to deal with her this early in the morning—at least not until after I'd been on the water.

"Got it last night," Olivia's clone, Marielle Davenport, replies. "What are you going to wear?"

"Well, Charlie likes it when I wear something that shows off my legs," Olivia says. She comes into view around the corner, flicking her long blonde hair over her shoulder. "So I'll probably wear something short, or at least something with a thigh-high slit." She titters, checking her nails.

Charlie.

Even at four o'clock in the goddamn morning, Olivia is name-dropping the Crown Prince of Farcliff. She talks about him as if they're engaged already, even though Dahlia told me Olivia has only met him once before at a state event four years ago. Olivia's father is the Prime Minister of Brundle, our neighbors to the south, so not only is she supremely annoying, but she's also been told that she's important since the day she was born.

Wonderful.

I tie my shoelaces loosely, knowing I'll take them off as soon as my boat is in the water. I stand up, and Olivia steps into my path.

"Did you get your invitation to the Prince's Ball, Elle?" She arches her perfectly groomed eyebrow and taps the side of her face with a manicured finger.

I don't answer.

"Is that a no?" Olivia glances at Marielle, grinning, before turning back to me. "Oh, right, you're just here as a charity case." She laughs, and Marielle follows suit.

I try to step around Olivia, but she moves with me. Her expensive perfume wafts toward me as she blocks my path. She's infuriating—right down to her long hair, curled into perfect, beachy waves that fall all the way down to her waist.

Seriously, who has time to curl their hair this early in the morning? I can just about manage to run a comb through my hair, and it's so short it barely gets tangled to begin with.

As I take another step to the side, Olivia mirrors my movements again to stop me.

"What, cat got your tongue?"

"I just want to practice, Olivia. You already know I haven't gotten an invite to that stupid party."

Marielle snorts. *Her* beachy blonde waves are already tied back in a high ponytail. The look she gives me is just as withering as Olivia's. "Stupid party? Elle, this isn't a 'stupid party'. This is where Prince Charlie chooses a wife."

I bite back my laughter, looking between the two of them. Everyone talks about the Prince's twenty-fifth birthday ball as if it's some magical, mystical, marriage-inducing event.

It's a freaking party—and a pretentious one at that.

Marielle and Olivia blink, staring at me.

"Wait, what? Are you being serious?" I scoff. "He chooses

a wife at this ball? Is this the Middle Ages? It's his birthday party."

They roll their eyes in unison, like two creepy plastic dolls.

"Fucking peasants," Olivia says, finally brushing past me. She takes care not to let any part of her body touch any part of mine, as if I'm some diseased leper.

"Pathetic. Of course she wouldn't understand, Ollie, she's from Grimdale." Marielle turns her big blue eyes to me. "Things are done differently in Farcliff, Elle. We actually have this thing called *class*. You should look it up."

She saunters past me without another look.

Rage.

My blood boils. My face turns beet red. Every stupid day of every stupid week, I'm made to feel like *less*. Less womanly. Less intelligent. Less worthy. Just... *less.*

Grimdale is only half an hour's drive away, but I might as well be from another planet for the way I'm treated here. It's not just Olivia and Marielle, either. All my teammates never waste an opportunity to make me feel like I don't belong here —like working my ass off for this stupid scholarship was a waste of time, because I'll never be accepted into this world no matter how hard I try.

I stomp out of the locker room and down to the warm-up area, even though my body is already burning hot. Olivia and Marielle will take their time to change their clothes and re-apply their makeup.

Yes, they need to *re*-apply their makeup before dawn. I'll never understand it.

I'm not complaining, though. It'll give me time to warm up and make my way to the shells on my own.

I heave a single scull onto my shoulder and grab my oars. The weight of the boat is already starting to calm me down.

Thank goodness I row singles, because I might not be able to resist capsizing us if I had to share a boat with either of those two egotistical, uppity little turds.

Coach Bernard is already waiting at the pier. He watches me put the shell in the water and set the oars in place. I keep my head down, not wanting to look up at the massive, stone building across the lake. Farcliff Castle looms above me, visible from almost everywhere on the university grounds. It's just one more stark reminder of how much I don't belong here. I'll always be the orphan girl from Grimdale, even if I do get this expensive, overrated university degree.

Coach clears his throat. "Everything okay?"

"Everything's fucking peachy, Coach." I kick my shoes off and set them on the shore before walking back toward my shell. My boat shoes are waiting for me at the end of the timber pier.

Coach looks at me under his dark, wiry eyebrows. He's assessing me—mentally, physically, emotionally—just like he does with all his athletes. I take a deep breath and square my shoulders, meeting his steely gaze. He drills his eyes into mine for a moment, then nods and looks down at his clipboard, satisfied.

"We're going for a steady, long interval practice today, Elle." Coach checks his notes.

I sweep my hand through my short brown hair, pushing it off my forehead. Between last night's sex party in Dahlia's room and this morning's encounter with the evil blonde twins, I'm having trouble focusing.

"Nice and easy," he continues. "I want you doing nine-minute 2k intervals. We're doing ten of them, so I hope you're nice and rested. It's going to be a long practice today. Here." He hands me the small headset I wear to hear his commands.

I slip my boat shoes on and get into the shell. The boat

rocks from side to side and I take a deep breath to calm myself down. The last thing I need is a dip in the lake at this hour.

When I'm set up near the marker buoys, I look up at Coach Bernard. His voice comes through the headset. *"All ready..."*

I grip the oars and close my eyes for the briefest moment. Inhaling deeply, I take in the scent of the water and the smell of the trees that line the shore. I savor the fresh, crisp taste of the air as it fills my lungs. My shell feels steady beneath me. My muscles coil in anticipation as I wait for my coach's command.

"Row."

My oars bite the water.

This is where I'm meant to be. I may be from Grimdale, and I may never get fancy little invitations to fancy little parties. I know I'll never become 'Charlie's' wife—or even see the Prince face-to-face—but I can row.

As my shell shears through the water, my whole body moves in sync—from my breath, through every muscle, and right down to the boat that supports me.

My height doesn't bother me here. On the water, it's an advantage. With every breath, I pull the oars through the water and sweep them back again, the blades almost skimming the glassy surface of Farcliff Lake. My body folds and extends with each stroke, and I'm free.

If I could fly, I imagine it would feel like this. It's effortless, smooth.

It's magic.

The air rushes around my body as my blood starts to pump. After two minutes, I'm nice and warm and I find my rhythm.

And I soar.

"*Wave left*," Coach says in my ear as a power boat passes by, leaving a wake for me to deal with. It doesn't bother me—I'm in my element. This is what I was made to do.

I was born to row.

By the eight-minute mark, my breath is ragged and my legs and arms are screaming with that sweet, sharp burn that I've grown addicted to. I must be close to the 2000-meter mark by now.

"*Three hundred.*"

I pull, and I forget about the lack of sleep and the harpies in the locker room. I forget about Dahlia and the fact that her healthy sex life is the exact opposite of my own nun-like existence. I even forget that I wish it wasn't.

I just do what I do best. I row.

ALSO BY LILIAN MONROE

For all books, visit:

www.lilianmonroe.com

Brother's Best Friend Romance

Shouldn't Want You

Can't Have You

Don't Need You

Won't Miss You

Military Romance

His Vow

His Oath

His Word

The Complete Protector Series

Enemies to Lovers Romance

Hate at First Sight

Loathe at First Sight

Despise at First Sight

The Complete Love/Hate Series

Secret Baby/Accidental Pregnancy Romance:

Knocked Up by the CEO

Knocked Up by the Single Dad

Knocked Up...Again!

Knocked Up by the Billionaire's Son

The Complete Unexpected Series

Bad Prince

Heartless Prince

Cruel Prince

Broken Prince

Wicked Prince

Wrong Prince

Fake Engagement/ Fake Marriage Romance:

Engaged to Mr. Right

Engaged to Mr. Wrong

Engaged to Mr. Perfect

Mr Right: The Complete Fake Engagement Series

Mountain Man Romance:

Lie to Me

Swear to Me

Run to Me

The Complete Clarke Brothers Series

Extra-Steamy Rock Star Romance:

Garrett

Maddox

Carter

The Complete Rock Hard Series

Made in the USA
Las Vegas, NV
19 October 2021

32654404R00095